There's something in the woods. . . .

I froze in my tracks.

"Do you hear that?" I whispered to Brooke. "Someone's coming toward us."

Now we *both* froze in our tracks. Someone was walking slowly and steadily through the trees. Making straight for us.

He wasn't making any effort to walk quietly, and the old leaves left over from the winter were rustling under his feet.

"Who's there?" I called out.

No one replied, but the walking continued.

Step. Step. Step. It was much closer now.

The steps stopped.

Suddenly, a streak of black flashed before my eyes. A huge black shape hurtled through the air toward me. And the next thing I knew, I was being grabbed by a tall, black-dressed figure whose pointed teeth were only inches from my throat.

Books by Ann Hodgman

My Babysitter Is A Movie Monster

Ann Hodgman

Illustrated by

John Pierard

iBooks for Young Readers
Habent Sua Fata Libelli

iBooks
Manhanset House
Dering Harbor, New York 11965

bricktower@aol.com • www.ibooksinc.com

Text and Illustrations Copyright © 1991 by General Licensing Company, Inc.
MY BABYSITTER is a trademark of Byron Preiss Visual Publications

Library of Congress Cataloging-in-Publication Data
Hodgman, Ann. My babysitter is a movie monster.
        (My babysitter) "A Byron Preiss book."
p. cm.
        [1. Young Adult Fiction—Horror. 2. Young Adult Fiction—Vampires
3. Young Adult Fiction—Thrillers & Suspense I. Hodgman, Ann, ill. II.
Title. III. Series: Hodgman, Ann. My babysitter.

ISBN 978-1-59687-647-7
2025

My Babysitter Is A Movie Monster

Table of Contents

Prologue

A hand, grayish-white and clawed, picks up a snapshot and holds it to the window.

Moonlight streams through the lead-paned glass and illuminates the picture of a girl about twelve or thirteen years old. Ski poles in hand, she's standing in front of a huge, craggy, snowcovered slope. There's a smile on her face, and her cheeks are ruddy with cold.

Written on the back of the picture, in a strange, craggy script, are the words "Meg Swain—Drazylvonia."

For the hundredth time the dark figure in the room studies Meg's face. If hatred could shrivel a photograph, it would. *I've wanted to kill this girl since I first laid eyes on her,* the figure thinks. *So harmless. So innocent.*

And yet this innocent human child has laid waste a whole vampire dynasty. This innocent human child has ruined plans that were centuries in the making. This innocent human child must be destroyed. . . .

Savagely the figure claws the picture to shreds.

Chapter One

January

"But, Meg, I have nothing to write *about*," moaned my father. He sounded like a kid with an overdue book report.

I sighed patiently. When Dad gets into his Ican't-write mood, you have to jolly him out of it.

"Why don't you write something about when you were a kid?" I suggested.

"Nothing happened during my childhood," Dad grumped. "I sat quietly with my hands folded the whole time." He turned back to his computer screen and typed a few lines. But when I bent over his shoulder to see what he'd written, all I saw was something beginning, "Ydpujlkg kjtlkjg sl ytj."

"I'm exercising my fingers," my father explained sheepishly. "It'll help the ideas come faster."

I decided not to argue. Dad's the creative one, not me.

Of course, he wasn't being very creative at that moment, which is why he had called me into his office. My father is a screenwriter. He writes for the movies and for TV, and he thinks every single project he works on is the hardest thing he's ever done. Now he was supposed to be coming up with a made-for-TV movie that would appeal to both grown-ups and kids. Naturally, it was the hardest thing he had ever done.

So I was trying to help him come up with ideas.

"What about . . . uh . . . a family getting trapped in an avalanche?" I suggested. My own family had just spent Christmas vacation in the snowy mountains of Drazylvonia, so avalanches were still on my mind. We hadn't gotten trapped in one, although some other scary stuff had happened on that vacation—but I won't go into that now.

Dad shook his head. "There've been a lot of avalanche movies already."

"Giant slugs attack a town in Delaware?" I said. We live in Delaware ourselves.

Dad shook his head again. "The one giant slug in Delaware is sitting right here at his computer."

"Okay, how about . . . a seventh-grade girl with a vampire babysitter?"

At that moment a shadow seemed to pass across the window. I turned to see what it was, but there was nothing there.

"A vampire babysitter," he said thoughtfully. "That's got some possibilities."

"It does?" I asked blankly.

"Yup. You've got a good imagination, Meg."

He was right. I do have a good imagination. But my imagination hadn't dreamed up this idea. Two summers before, I'd actually *had* a vampire babysitter. And I didn't need to use my imagination to picture what the experience had been like. I could remember every detail.

If you already know about me, then you already know about my vampire babysitter, and you can skip this part. If you've never heard of me, then you're not going to believe this part, but you'd better pay attention anyway. Because every idea I gave my father for his screenplay was *my* story. It had all happened to me. . . .

"Vampire babysitter," Dad said firmly. He typed the words onto his computer screen, then looked hopefully at me. "What would he be like? What are his characteristics?"

"He could be a teenager. Someone like Vincent Graver," I said. "Remember how weird *he* was?"

"You thought so, anyway," said my dad. "Okay. A character like Vincent is a good starting point." He typed some more. Then, once again, he looked up at me expectantly.

"You want me to come up with the whole story?" I asked.

"No, no. Just—just let's brainstorm a little." (Brainstorming is what Dad calls making other people think up ideas and then stealing them.) "Who should this vampire be babysitting for?"

Well, that wasn't hard.

"How about a girl like me?" I suggested, or rather pretended to suggest. "Someone who's really too old for a babysitter, but her parents insist she needs one anyway because they don't trust her. You know, the way you and Mom used to be." *If only the two of you had realized I was old enough to take care of myself—and Trevor— Vincent Graver would never have come into our lives in the first place*, I added silently.

Trevor is my younger brother. Vincent Graver is—well, was—our sixteen-year-old vampire babysitter. My parents hired him a couple of summers ago. I realized he was a vampire pretty quickly, but it took most of that summer to get rid of him. Unfortunately, the "getting rid of" was only temporary. Vincent came right back the following summer. My brother and I got rid of him again, but he kept turning up. Most recently, I had actually gone to *his* home in the Carpathian Mountains. (That's another story, too.) After that we'd made a temporary truce—not that I could really trust a *vampire* to keep his side of a bargain.

Of course, my father knew nothing about this. He and Mom hadn't noticed anything wrong with Vincent.

"Boy, you sure used to squawk about having to have a sitter," Dad said now. "It's not that Mom and I didn't trust you, Meg. We just wanted to make sure that—well, let's not start all over again. Let's go on with this screenplay. Okay, the vampire is babysitting for a girl your age. What's our setting?"

"How about a place like Moose Island?" I said.

Wait—there *was* something at the window. I had definitely seen it that time. A shadow, a vague outline?

No. The window was empty.

"What's the matter?" asked my father.

"I—Nothing. I thought there was someone looking in through the window, that's all." I shivered. "I guess this idea's getting to me. Anyway, what was I saying? Oh, yes. That the story could be set on a place like Moose Island."

Moose Island, which is off the coast of Maine, is the place my family spends the summers. Vincent Graver had brought his coffin to Moose Island on the ferry and set up housekeeping there. When Mom met him, she thought he was so charming that she hired him to take care of me and my brother. So much for a mother's instincts.

Dad was nodding now. "There'd be a lot of good locations on an island," he said. "Plenty of interesting places to film. The ocean, the woods, the town . . . But why would a vampire be living on an *island?*"

"Because there's a bloodbank at the hospital," I blurted out. "Vampires have to go where the blood is, you know."

Was that someone *tapping* on the window? No, it couldn't be. I took a deep breath and started in with my story. While my father sat typing as fast as he could, I "suggested" my whole story to him.

How the girl my age ("I think I'll just go ahead and call her Meg," Dad said) had started to suspect there was something wrong with a babysitter who had pointed teeth and no reflection in mirrors. How the girl's suspicions had been confirmed (kind of dramatically) when the babysitter turned into a bat and bit her on the neck. How she had set out to get the vampire off the island and finally succeeded—or so she thought. Because it had turned out that vampires are even harder to get rid of than the books tell you. . . .

"It's *fantastic*, Meg," my father said when I was finished. "It'll make a great, great screenplay. Let's give it a working title. How about Terror *Summer*?" He studied the monitor for a second. "But you know, I think it would work even better if the vampire was a bear."

"A bear," I repeated tonelessly.

"Uh-huh. Here's how I see it." Dad's eyes were shining with excitement. "Meg suspects that a bear is living in the woods, but no one believes her because there've never been any bears on that island. He escaped from a zoo or something. Then it turns out that the bear is actually *stalking* Meg. Meg ends up making friends with the bear, of course, but she doesn't try to tame him because she knows he's meant to be wild. In the end—let's see—in the end maybe she ends up saving him from some angry townspeople.

"Animal stories arc always hits. I think this is really going to be great," Dad went on. "Thanks so much for getting me started, Meggie. What would I do without you?"

"I have absolutely no idea," I muttered.

It must have been a month or so later that the phone rang during dinner. My brother Trevor and I practically knocked over the kitchen table trying to get to the phone first, but unfortunately it was for Dad. We sat down disappointedly and went back to fighting about whose turn it was to clean out our cat Pooch's litter box. Before we could settle that interesting point, Dad let out a whoop of joy.

"You do? That's great! You are? Great? *Here?* That's great! Wow, that's really great! She can? Because it's her spring break—that will be perfect. It was all her idea, you know. Great! Fantastic!" he added, for some variety. "Okay, we'll be in touch. That's really, really great!"

"What's great?" asked Trevor the instant Dad hung up.

"Well, the producers *loved* my script," Dad exulted. "They're calling it *My Babysitter Is a Vampire.*"

"What vampire?" I asked. "I thought you changed the vampire to a bear."

"Oh, I changed it back," said Dad carelessly. "I couldn't get the bear to do what I wanted. So we're back to your original idea, Meg. And wait, it gets better. They're actually going to film the script right here in Delaware—about half an hour away from our house."

"But it all happened on Moose Island!" I protested without thinking.

"I know, but movie producers never do things just the way you expect. They decided an island would be too complicated. So now they'll just film everything here on the Atlantic coast and *pretend* it's an island."

"That's great, Dad," I said politely.

"No, it's *really* great," he corrected me. "Because they want me on the set as a consultant. And they're shooting during your spring break, Meg. You can come along with me. I told the director you helped come up with the idea. Bring Brooke, too—the director said you can bring a friend.

They might even let the two of you be extras in a couple of scenes if you want!"

"If we *want?*" I echoed incredulously. "Of course we want! Dad, how—how great!" Brooke Donahue was my best friend. And I was *sure* she'd be as excited about this as I was.

Then I suddenly remembered that I have a brother, and at that moment he was looking a little droopy. I couldn't really blame him. "What about Trevor?" I asked. "Doesn't he get to come?"

"I think this would be a perfect time to take Trevor on a little trip by himself," my mother put in. "You and Dad will be so busy that we'd be bored staying at home. We'll figure something out."

"How about the Himalayas?" my brother asked excitedly. "We could track down a yeti!"

I could see that he'd stopped feeling droopy, but I decided that it *was* my turn to clean out the cat litter after all. When you've just gotten really good news, you can breeze through gross jobs.

Later that evening my father came into my room and held out a stack of paper.

"I didn't want to show you this unless the producers liked it," he said. "But now—since you're the one who thought up the whole idea—I thought you might like to take a look."

It was a copy of his screenplay. Across the top, Dad had scribbled its new title: my babysitter is a vampire.

"See what you think," said Dad. "If you have any suggestions, I'd love to hear them—not that I'll pay attention." He grinned at me and left.

This was a good excuse not to finish the homework that was spread out all over my bed. I shuffled all my papers into a pile, picked up the screenplay, scrunched my pillow into a comfortable shape, and started reading out loud.

"*Act 1, Scene 1. Ext.*" (That meant "exterior," I knew.) "*Pan in on a crowded ferry dock from which a ferry is pulling off into a thick fog. Newly arrived vacationers, struggling with luggage, are beginning to file down the dock toward the island.*

"*We now notice a very tall, very cadaverous-looking boy, perhaps sixteen years old, who is making his way through the crowd. His skin is a ghastly grayish-white except for his lips, which are a dull maroon. He is dressed entirely in black; his black eyes stare ahead without expression. CLOSE-UP as he licks his lips, revealing pointed teeth. He bends down and hoists something heavy onto his shoulder, then slowly begins moving through the crowd. He is staggering under the weight of his burden—a large black coffin. . . .*"

I couldn't believe it. This was Vincent *exactly* as I had first seen him. My father had gotten every single detail right. And I hadn't told him any of that stuff.

As I sat there brooding over this, I thought I saw *another* flicker at the window. *But I couldn't have!* I said to myself. *My bedroom's on the second floor of the house. No one could look in my window up here.*

Could they?

No, of course not. . . .

I read a little further—far enough to see that my father was still, creepily, exactly on track. Practically *everything* in the screenplay was identical to what had happened to me. Through what seemed more like magic than anything else, he had taken the skeleton of a story I'd given him and turned it into my own eerie past.

As I read on, I actually started to get scared. The story was so real that I felt as though I were living it all over again.

Once more I suffered through the terrors I'd felt when I was hunting down Vincent. The dead-of-night search for his hut—the terrible moment when he had reared up out of his coffin and grabbed me—the anguished race for safety with Vincent just behind me . . . All of these came back to . . . well . . . to haunt me.

What was going to happen to the screenplay Meg? My heart thudded as I read. Would she be okay, or would she end up in the screenplay Vincent's clutches?

When I had finished reading, I collapsed back onto my bed with relief. Meg did end up safe— at least for the moment.

We see the ferry pulling away just in time, Dad had written. *Meg leans against the railing, watching as the sun's first rays strike Vincent square in the face. CLOSEUP on Vincent's howl of agony. He disappears beneath the water's surface. CLOSEUP on Meg, who is laughing and crying with relief.*

Well, I was going to insist that Dad change the laughing-and-crying part. I'm not *that* much of a sap.

But the story had come out okay. I could stop being scared now . . . which left me free to wonder just exactly what was going on with my bedroom window.

You know the feeling you get when someone's staring at you? I'm sure it's happened to you. You can't see anything, but you can *sense* something.

When that happens to me, I usually turn around to find my cat trying to hypnotize me. *It's time to eat. It's time to eat,* he's telling me. (No matter what time it is, Pooch always thinks it's time to eat.)

But this time I could see Pooch out in the hall. He was sound asleep on the pile of clean clothes I was supposed to bring into my room but hadn't yet.

It wasn't Pooch staring at me, then. And yet the feeling was very, very strong. I stared at my window again.

Were my curtains moving now? Had an invisible hand reached in and tugged them?

"Yeah, right," I scoffed out loud.

Then I heard the same tapping I'd heard downstairs in my father's office. Someone really *was* tapping at my window. A thin, dry tapping, like something that came from a long, pointed fingernail.

Or just from a branch, I reminded myself stoutly. I counted to three in my head. Then I steeled myself, jumped up, and walked right over to my window.

Something darted out of sight just as I got there. Or I thought it did. But down below, my street lay quiet and empty and motionless. If anything was out there, it was hiding in the shadows now.

But that was a big *if.* Why should there be anything out there? How could there be anything out there? *You're getting too imaginative,* I scolded myself. *What could it be—a giant slug! Think about something else for a change.*

So I decided to think about who was going to play me in the movie.

It never occurred to me that the movie and the disturbance at my window had any connection.

How could I have known that putting my story on film was going to unleash a new evil force . . . and plunge me into the worst danger I had ever faced?

Chapter Two

Spring break, six weeks later

The Delaware seashore

My introduction to the glamorous world of moviemaking was not all I had hoped.

"Hi, I'm Meg Swain. How do you do?" I said, stepping forward to shake hands with the first person Dad took me over to. She had reddish hair cropped above her shoulders, and she was standing next to some kind of big camera thing.

"Watch out!" I heard someone behind me shout.

Too late. I tripped over a cord, wobbled sideways, banged into the big camera thing, knocked it over, fell backward, and landed on something bumpy that turned out to be some kind of *small* camera thing that was lying on the ground.

"How do *you* do?" said the woman with short red hair, politely going back to the last thing I'd said before I started destroying things. "My name is Nora Kilmer. People just call me Kilmer."

"Kilmer the Killer," said a man next to her with a chuckle.

"That's what they say," the red-haired woman agreed with a grimace. "Anyway, you must be the one who thought up this story. I'm directing the movie your dad wrote."

"Oh, no!" I wailed, staggering to my feet. "The director—and the first thing I do is break your camera! It must be worth a million dollars!"

Nora Kilmer laughed politely. "Not quite that much. And the camera's pretty tough. I'm sure it's not broken." But she didn't look a hundred percent sure. . . .

It was the first day of spring break—and the third day of production for *My Babysitter Is a Vampire*. Dad, Brooke, and I had just arrived on the set, which in this case meant a deserted beach an hour south of my house, and Dad was introducing us around. Naturally I wanted to make a good impression.

And I had succeeded. Or at least I had made an impression. Or at least I had gotten everyone within a two-mile radius to notice me. And laugh at me. Which is *sort* of good, isn't it? There's not enough laughter in this world, my mom always says. (She also says the reason I'm so clumsy these days is that I'm growing so fast. Which is not exactly a comforting thought, considering that I'm already taller than most of the boys in my class.) And right at that moment I wished that I was *with* my mom, who had taken Trevor to nice, faraway, unembarrassing Disney World.

Anyway, it was a damp, foggy day—so foggy, in fact, that the people on the set, and all their cameras and equipment, were walled by mist into a little world of their own. Behind us I could hear the ocean, but I could hardly see it. Not that I could have seen much at that point. I was too busy trying to stop blushing.

Kilmer was shaking hands with Brooke now. (No problems there! Brooke *never* makes a fool of herself.) Kilmer seemed to be in her thirties. Other than that, though, she looked pretty cool. I don't know how movie directors usually dress, but Kilmer was wearing black jeans, a black linen blazer, a black T-shirt, and black combat boots.

"Everyone looks so regular," Brooke whispered to me as Dad and Kilmer exchanged hellos. "I thought it would be more movieish."

I knew what she meant. I was a little disappointed, too—even though of course being here was better than being in school. I'd been hoping to see guys running around yelling "Cut!" and one of those huge fans they use to make it look windy on a set, and maybe even a beautiful movie star in a sequined gown, though I don't know where *she* would have fit into the story. But the people here were just ordinary grown-ups dressed for a chilly March day at the beach. Some of them were holding complicated camera-related machines—as you've probably realized by now, I'm not great at describing machines— some of them were holding clipboards, but most of them were just standing around.

Then I caught sight of the girl right behind Kilmer—a girl who looked exactly like Brooke. For a few confused seconds I wondered why Brooke had changed her clothes. (Brooke was wearing a polar fleece jacket, jeans, and sneakers. The "other" Brooke was wearing a quilted floweredsilk jacket, matching leggings, and suede boots.) Then I realized that Brooke was still standing next to me. And that this girl was a brunette, not a redhead like Brooke. The Brooke behind Kilmer could have been Brooke's double.

Like Brooke, the other girl had long, curly hair. Both girls had the same ruddy complexions. They even had identical *noses*. I couldn't believe it.

"Who are you?" I blurted out.

Brooke's clone looked closely at me and smiled. "I'm you."

"What?" I blurted even more dopily. It was only nine in the morning, and already this day was too hard for me.

Now the girl laughed. "I should have said, I'm *playing* you. My name is Gabrielle Tumolo. I'm going to be Meg in the movie."

"You are? Wow, what a compliment! I mean, you don't even look like me." (I'm not ugly, but I'm awfully average.) "You should really be playing Brooke."

"We didn't choose Gabrielle for her looks," Kilmer told me. "It was her talent we noticed. She just turned up at a casting call. A total unknown—and she blew us all away."

"Stop!" protested Gabrielle. "You'll jinx me."

"I doubt it," said Kilmer, giving Gabrielle a friendly cuff on the shoulder. "You're unjinxable. As I'm sure Brooke and Meg will find out.

Anyway, we've been wasting time too long." Kilmer was suddenly all business, though we'd actually only been standing around for about four minutes. "Let's do a run-through of the scene where Meg's parents tell her about her new babysitter. Places, everyone!"

When he had first gotten the news about *My Babysitter Is a Vampire*, Dad had told me a little about how the movie was going to be made. I knew it wasn't going to be one of those action pictures where they spend a bajillion dollars to make the heroine sprout wings or something. Kilmer only had a week and a half to shoot the whole thing. To make things even more complicated, the little town where the beach scenes were being filmed had only allowed the film crew to shoot in early spring.

The scene the actors were about to rehearse now—the first in the screenplay—was supposed to take place at a picnic on the beach. Since this was just a quick run-through, we wouldn't have to watch Gabrielle and her "parents" shivering through the scene in their bathing suits. It wasn't too bad for March, but I thought that all three of them looked a little chilly as they sat down on the sand and pretended to be unpacking a picnic basket.

I can't tell you how weird it felt to watch people pretending to be me and my parents. The actors playing Gabrielle's mom and dad looked nothing like *my* mom and dad. They didn't act like my parents, either. The dad in the movie was one of those gruff-yet-twinkly pipe-smoking types. The actor playing him had come up with tons of little mannerisms that were supposed to say "I'm a writer." He kept glancing up at the sky as if searching for inspiration. Then he'd give an "Ah, I've got it!" nod and scribble imaginary words on an imaginary notepad. If my father ever tried that, we'd mock him for the rest of his life.

The movie mom, who looked about twenty years younger than a real mother of a seventh grader, kept checking her watch all the time. In fact, that was the first reason Kilmer stopped the rehearsal.

"Caryl, are you late for something?" she asked.

"Oh, no, no, no! This is part of my interpretation. I'm trying to convey how busy the mother is," the movie Mom said earnestly. "How she's so terribly guilty about having to hire a babysitter, but really feels she has no choice with all her important medical studies. Having her check her watch gives us more insight into her conflicts."

I thought I saw Kilmer stifle a sigh. "Well, that's an interesting idea. Try to keep it to a minimum, though," she said. "Okay, let's start again from the top."

That's one thing Dad hadn't prepared me for: how many, many times they started the scene over. Whenever any of the actors managed to squeeze out more than a syllable or two, Kilmer would find a reason to stop them.

"But, *Mom!*" Gabrielle protested at one point in the scene. "You're being so unfair! No one else my age has a—"

"Gabby," Kilmer interrupted, "let's see how it would work if you clasp your hands while you're talking. You know, as if you're *begging* her to listen to you."

Gabrielle squeezed her hands together in front of her. "But, *Mom!*" she burst out again. "You're being so unf—"

"No, I guess that doesn't work," said Kilmer briskly. "It looks as if you're praying to her. Try it again, without the hands."

That kind of thing happened over and over. When Kilmer wasn't making suggestions of her own, she was fending off suggestions from Caryl, the actress playing the mother. "I think it would be a way in for the audience if the mother has hysterics at this line," Caryl offered at one point. With all the stops and interruptions, it took more than two hours to "run through" a scene that took up two pages in the screenplay. Maybe it should have been called a walkaround, not a runthrough. By the time Kilmer was finally satisfied, all three actors looked exhausted—and Brooke and I were bored out of our minds. All *we'd* been doing was standing there watching.

"That was fine," Kilmer told the actors. "Exactly right. Now take a break, and then we'll try the next scene."

Gabrielle groaned. "Kilmer, it's almost lunchtime! Can't we eat first? I'm starving."

Kilmer frowned. "Why does everyone always get hungry?" she asked impatiently. "It's such a waste of time! Okay, we'll pick up with the next scene after lunch."

"Lunch," Gabrielle announced, walking up to me and Brooke, "is the high point of my day. And dinner, too, of course. Shall we go see what they've got for us?"

I looked around for my dad, but he was nowhere to be seen. I figured he must be off working somewhere, so Brooke and I quickly agreed. I thought it was nice of Gabrielle not to be movie-star-ish. She could have stuck around with the other actors, after all.

We picked our way across the damp sand toward a small picnic pavilion at the end of the beach. Gabrielle smiled when she saw the pavilion. "Good! The caterers have already put out our lunch. It feels like five hundred years since I had breakfast."

The main picnic table in the pavilion was covered with big platters of food, and all the people who'd been standing around on the beach were now standing in line to fill their plates. Everything looked fantastic. Brooke and I both crammed as much food onto our plates as we could (continuing in my clod mode, I dumped a steaming splat of lasagna onto the table), but Gabrielle only took a milkshake that some woman handed her.

"That's your lunch?" I asked. "A strawberry milkshake?"

"It's not a regular milkshake. It's a protein diet shake. I have to stay skinny this week," Gabrielle answered with a sigh. She took a thirsty slurp from her straw, draining half the cup. "This has everything I need in it, but it's not as good as real food. Believe me, if we weren't shooting, I'd be totally pigging out. Let's eat in the trailer," Gabrielle went on. "It's too cold out here."

It was true that the people hunched around the picnic tables looked pretty miserable despite the great food. I could see that it wasn't only the actors who would suffer from working outside in March. Everyone on the crew was stuck outside as well. As far as I was concerned, the glamour of the movie business was starting to wear off.

Gabrielle led us toward the parking lot, where a rather battered-looking trailer was parked.

"Home sweet home," she said wryly. "All the actors have to share the same one. The producers are saving money."

"You're all *sleeping* in that thing?" asked Brooke.

"Oh, no. We're staying in a hotel in town. The trailer's just where we get to rest between shots and where they do our makeup and costumes and stuff. If we ever get to that point," she added ruefully. "Kilmer is kind of a perfection-ist."

We'd reached the trailer now. Gabrielle pulled open the door and gestured us in ahead of her. But I didn't get to see what was inside.

As the door opened, a bloodcurdling howl ripped through the air. It was followed by the slow, ominous tread of heavy footsteps coming from inside the trailer.

"Th-there's someone inside," I said nervously.

Before Gabrielle could answer, another howl hurled it-self toward us. The footsteps were so heavy that I could *see* the trailer shaking.

Then a hideous black-shrouded figure appeared in the doorway.

"A vampire!" Brooke whispered.

Yes. It was a vampire. His clawed hands were raised high over his head. His mouth gaped open, and I saw that he had gleaming fangs instead of teeth.

I barely had time to notice the blood oozing from his mouth before he threw himself at my throat.

Chapter Three

I heard someone screaming for help, but I don't know who it was. Everything was happening too fast.

The vampire crashed into me, knocking me to the ground. Gasping for breath, I tried to struggle to my feet—but he was too fast for me. Kneeling above me, he wrapped his hands around my neck and began to squeeze. Now his horrible face was only inches from mine—a pale green face, with strangely blue eyes. And now black dots were swirling around in front of me. I was starting to pass out. . . .

"Oh, Mortimer, cut that out. You're such a bore."

It was Gabrielle's voice, sharp with annoyance.

The hands let go. I fell to the ground again, landing on my plate, which had fallen the first time I did. This was quite a day for things hitting the ground.

"I was *rehearsing*," said the vampire. "I have to stay in *character*, Gabby. You know that."

I shook my head to clear it. This vampire sounded like an ordinary boy. A *whiny* ordinary boy, not more than sixteen. And suddenly that's what he looked like, too.

Now I could see that his greenish skin was pasty in some spots. It was just makeup, amateurishly applied. And his black cape was really an old black coat. (Up close I could see the frayed edges where the sleeves had been cut off and clumsily sewn shut.) And the claws on his hands were the kind you buy in a bag and stick onto your fingers.

"Meg, Brooke, this is Mortimer Mainwaring." Gabrielle's voice was disgusted. "My, uh, co-star in the movie. He plays Vincent. All the time."

The vampire smirked. "Just being professional, ladies." He swept a gallant bow in my direction. "Sorry if I upset you."

"Upset me!" I repeated furiously. "You try to kill me and then apologize for upsetting me?"

"I wasn't trying to kill you." Mortimer smirked again. "Just trying to scare you a bit. And you must admit, I did a good job."

"That's not professional." I could tell that Brooke was furious, too. "That's just obnoxious."

"Girls, girls," said Mortimer in an oily voice. "Let's forget about the past. I'm sure we all agree that the main thing is to put out the greatest film we can. Right?" Now he was all wide-eyed earnestness. "And if I got carried away, it's just because I care so much about this production."

"That's enough, Mortimer," came yet another voice—this time from behind me. I turned around and saw Nora Kilmer, the director. My dad was right behind her. They must have heard the scream and come to see what was the matter.

"Meg, Mortimer sometimes takes his part too seriously," Kilmer went on. "It can be disturbing to outsiders."

"I noticed."

I expected Kilmer to make Mortimer apologize. Instead, she said, "But I've got to say I liked the look of that little scene, Mortimer. It would be great to have Vincent jump out at Meg like that at some point during the story. I wonder if there's a place we could write it into the script." She turned to my father. "What do you think?"

"Uh—I'm not sure," Dad said slowly. "Vincent does leap out of his coffin at the end. Isn't that enough?"

"That's good, but I love the idea of him lurking behind a door somewhere and then flying out to attack Meg," Kilmer said. She gave my father what I can only describe as a firm look. "See what you can do, okay?"

In return Dad gave Kilmer a tired smile. "Okay. You're the director."

"But that's not fair," I objected. "Dad, you shouldn't have to change your screenplay just because of some stupid stunt Mortimer pulled."

He patted me on the shoulder. "It's all right, Meg. I'm used to making changes. Screenwriters have to do it all the time."

"Right," said Kilmer crisply. "We're all working together."

You sound like Mortimer, I thought. But I had enough sense not to say it aloud. Kilmer was in charge here, not Dad—and certainly not me.

She glanced around at us. "Everything settled? Good. Let's go back to work in five minutes."

For a moment the five of us stared at her back as she walked away. Then Gabrielle sighed.

"Well, I have five minutes left for lunch."

Of course *my* lunch was splattered all over the parking lot as well as all over me. But meeting Mortimer had pretty much killed my appetite.

"I'd better clean this mess up," I said.

"I'll help," Brooke said. "Do you have some paper towels?"

"Inside the trailer," Gabrielle said. "I'll show you."

Mortimer did not offer to help.

Well, it wasn't as if Mortimer Mainwaring was the first obnoxious kid I'd ever met. Yes, his constant leaping-out-of-corners routine got a little tiresome. Yes, his maniacal vampire laugh got old after I'd heard it a couple of hundred times. Yes, the way he dribbled blood capsules out of his mouth and constantly whooshed his cape around made me want to punch him in the face.

But Mortimer wasn't the only obnoxious person on the set. Caryl, who played Meg's mother, had plenty of obnoxious ideas of her own.

At one point they were rehearsing a scene where Meg's parents went out for the evening and left Meg alone with her vampire babysitter. (There was no Trevor character in this movie. The producers had gotten rid of him to save money.) In Dad's original version they just *went out for the evening*. No big deal. The important part of the story happened after they had left, when the vampire started prowling around Meg's house.

But Caryl thought that wasn't dramatic enough. In the middle of the rehearsal she suddenly stopped and stared up at the ceiling of the big old beach house the producers had rented. Her lips moved silently, as if she was talking to herself.

"'You're sure you're going to be okay, Meg?' " Gabrielle prompted her.

Caryl's lovely green eyes (I think she wore tinted contacts) looked shocked. "I haven't forgotten the line," she said. "I'm just considering something."

"Uh-oh," Dad whispered. He was standing just outside the door with Brooke and me, watching the rehearsal.

"Wouldn't the scene play better if we lock Meg in her room before we leave?" Caryl asked.

"Why would you do *that?*" asked Kilmer.

"Uh . . . Maybe Meg's being so rude about having a babysitter that we decide she needs to be punished," Caryl answered. "You know girls that age."

"I'm a girl that age!" I protested. I hated the thought of an actor trying to change what had really happened to me. "I wouldn't let anyone lock me in my room even if I deserved it! Which I wouldn't," I added.

Caryl didn't pay attention to us. She was staring up at the ceiling again.

A smoldering look of rage slowly began to spread across her perky face. Her nostrils flared, and she started breathing hard. Then she whipped around to face us.

"How *dare* you, Meg!" she shrieked. "You little wretch, you have no *right* to interfere in my plans!"

We all stared at her, appalled. I was the most shocked of all, since I was the one she was yelling at.

Or was I? Like a snake Caryl sprang forward and grabbed Gabrielle's arm. "I'm taking you up to your room, young lady," she growled between clenched teeth. "And I'm locking the door until you've thought over your misbehavior!"

Abruptly she dropped Gabby's arm and looked over at Kilmer. "Well, what do you think?" she asked. "How does it play?"

I realized I'd been holding my breath. Now I let it out. Caryl had been acting—not suddenly going crazy.

Kilmer pursed her lips consideringly. "Well, I'll think about it, Caryl," she said. "It would have to be toned down a little, but it might work."

"But it didn't *happen* that way!" I wailed. "I mean, my father didn't write it that way. He would never write something like that. It's—it's way over the top."

Kilmer frowned. "I don't recall anyone asking your opinion, Meg," she said sharply. "And actually it might be good to introduce a little more conflict at this point." She looked at my father.

"You're probably right," Dad said in a rather unthrilled voice. There was a pause. Then Dad brightened. "Come to think of it, having Meg locked in her room might be better. That way she'd be more trapped when Vincent came up looking for her. He could get in, but she couldn't get out—"

"Exactly," said Kilmer. "How long will it take to rewrite the scene?"

"I'll start right now," my father told her. "My laptop computer is out in the car. I'll just go get it."

"Great. We'll do a run-through of the next scene while you're working on this one."

"Thank you, everyone. I really think it will work much, much better now," Caryl said solemnly. "I get these little flashes of insight now and then—and do you know, they always turn out to be right?"

And do you know, I bet they always end up in your having more lines! I thought.

Over the next couple of hours Dad had to write a lot more changes—even though the script was supposed to be all done. He had to add a scene where Reid, the movie dad, did some repair work up on the roof of the house. ("I should look more involved in family life," Reid explained.) He had to *cut* a scene that Caryl thought made her sound unsympathetic. ("It's important for the audience to identify with me," Caryl explained.) He even had to give the cat in the movie more to do. ("Animal scenes are so popular with kids," Kilmer explained.)

Finally Dad asked for permission to work in a room at the hotel. "As long as I'm doing a whole rewrite, I'll get a lot more done off the set," he told Kilmer tactfully. I think he meant, "Because then no one could ask me to make more changes," but he didn't say that.

"It's fine with me," Kilmer said. "Do the girls want to stay here?"

"Yes," Brooke and I said in unison.

"I'll drop in to check on things every now and then. And I can pick them up at the end of the day," Dad suggested.

"It's okay with me. Just keep in the background, girls. Don't get in my way," said Kilmer bluntly.

When Dad was no longer around, Caryl had to find new ways of getting attention.

"That girl there is making me forget my lines," she suddenly announced in the middle of a rehearsal. She was frowning at me.

"Me?" I said, flustered. I had just been standing quietly in the background.

"Yes, you. You're making faces at me," said Caryl. "She waits until your back is turned, Kilmer, and then she starts in with some *very* ugly expressions. I think she's trying to break my concentration."

"Are you making faces, Meg?" asked Kilmer sternly.

"I don't think so," I answered in confusion.

"She's absolutely *grimacing* at me," Caryl insisted. "Do we really have to have all these children underfoot? It makes our working conditions so much worse."

"That's not fair!" Brooke put in loyally. "Meg isn't making faces."

"I haven't seen any, either," Gabrielle added.

"That's because she's not making faces at *you*," said Caryl spitefully. "Kilmer, I really can't put up with this much longer."

Kilmer was frowning. "Don't let her distract you," she told Caryl. Then she turned to me. "And Meg, why don't you just try to keep the expression off your face?"

"But I really wasn't—" I started.

"Forget it," Kilmer interrupted. "I'm not interested." She wasn't even looking at me anymore. "Now, where were we?"

"I really wasn't making faces, you know," I told Brooke in the car going home that night.

"I know you weren't," she said sympathetically. "Caryl's awful."

"Kilmer's not all that great, either," I said with a sigh.

"We could just stay home for a couple of days," Brooke suggested.

I glanced quickly up at my father. "I think that might hurt Dad's feelings," I said in a low voice. "He was so excited about our getting to come along." I sighed. "And I *know* this is going to start being fun really soon."

Considering how much *less* fun everything was about to become, that may have been the dumbest thing I ever said.

Chapter Four

Both Brooke and I were glad to see that things picked up on our third day. At the end of that day Kilmer announced that finally—*finally!*— they were going to start shooting actual scenes from the screenplay instead of just rehearsing all the time.

"We can only use the Fulton house for two more days," she told everyone. The Fulton house was the one they were renting for the scenes that showed "Meg's" beach house in the movie. "So we're going to try to shoot all the house scenes tomorrow and the next day."

Dad had already told me that movies are almost never filmed in sequence. The scenes are shot in whatever order is most convenient. All the beach scenes in *My Babysitter Is a Vampire* would be filmed together in a clump. ("Assuming the weather cooperates," said Dad.) All the house scenes would be shot at the same time, all the forest scenes would be shot at the same time, and so on. Then, at the end, everything would somehow get patched together into the right order. I was glad that the patching-together part wasn't my job. I don't even like doing puzzles.

"Actors, I need you here at six a.m. tomorrow for makeup," Kilmer went on.

None of the actors seemed surprised at this. They just nodded. Well, Mortimer also whooshed his cape around and muttered, "But of course, my dear." But no one paid any attention.

"Okay. That's it for today. See you *first thing* tomorrow." Kilmer sounded as strict as a teacher.

We got to the set at 6:30 the next morning. In the trailer the makeup artist had only just gotten started on Gabrielle and Mortimer.

A long mirror ran across one section of wall at the far end of the trailer. Mortimer's chair was positioned in the exact middle of the mirror. He was staring intently at his reflection as the makeup woman worked on him. You could tell he was watching her every move, waiting to pounce if she made a mistake.

"Left to right," he ordered. "Make sure you only put my makeup on from left to right."

"I've never heard of that," the woman said mildly.

"Well, you *obviously* don't keep up with the developments in your job, then!" grumbled Mortimer. "And I want you to make sure I'm pale enough. I must be *extraordinarily* white. *Ghastly* white."

The woman sighed. "Okay, sweetie. I'll make you as ghastly as I can."

"I have to be sure," Mortimer insisted. "Move my chair closer to the mirror so I can see myself better. No! *Closer!*"

"I don't know why're you're making such a fuss," Gabrielle said. She was leaning back in a chair in the corner, her eyes half-closed, drinking some of her diet shake. A second makeup artist, this one a young man with a waist-length ponytail, was applying tiny clumps of false eyelashes to her eyelids. "I don't even want to see myself. I hate the way I look in makeup. Besides, these people know what they're doing."

Mortimer gave one of his oily smirks. "Yes, as long as a professional keeps an eye on them."

"Okay, Mortimer," said his makeup artist again, before Gabrielle got the chance to answer. "I'm going to need you to keep quiet for a few minutes, dear. I have to do your fangs."

This seemed like a good time for me to announce myself. "Hi, Gabrielle," I said. "I don't know if you can see us. It's Meg and Brooke. Are you excited about today?"

Gabrielle peered over at us as best she could with someone yanking her eyelids around. "Kind of," she said. "Knowing that I'm going to be doing all this stuff in front of a camera makes it seem a lot more real, somehow."

"*I'm* mop mermush," Mortimer said from his chair at the other end of the trailer.

"What?" said Brooke.

"I *fed*, I'm mop—"

"I think he's saying he's not nervous," translated the woman who was doing his makeup. "But, Mortimer, honey, you really shouldn't talk until I've finished with these fangs."

That was good news.

"You're almost done, Gabby," said her makeup artist. "I didn't have to do much in the way of foundation. You've got a great tan already." He reached for a hand mirror. "Want to take a look at the finished product?"

Gabrielle shuddered. "No, thanks," she said. "I told you already, I feel stupid walking around like this. I don't mean to be rude," she added quickly. "I'm sure you've done a great job." She turned to me and Brooke. "Want to go over to the set?"

We nodded.

"I wish I could join you, ladies," Mortimer butted in, "but it takes so long to get my look just right. Move me closer to the mirror," he commanded again. He gave a loud, mournful sigh. "Why am I surrounded with such *incompetent* people? I'll probably be here for *hours.*"

"Thank goodness for that," muttered Gabrielle as we left the trailer and headed across the lawn to the front of the Fulton house. "Wow, what a great place," she added, gesturing at the house. "If I ever make a lot of money, I'm going to buy one just like it."

The Fulton house was a mansion, really—a mammoth white building with six chimneys. The whole outside of the house was cluttered with cameras and light meters and sound equipment and people walking around taking notes, but I was so used to them by now that I could look right through them to the house itself. It was two hundred years old, and it made my family's real beach house in Maine look like a plywood birdhouse.

I tipped my head back to see the house's top story. It was ringed by a widow's walk. Have you ever seen one? A widow's walk is one of those balconies that wrap around the whole top story of a house. In the olden days, sea captains' wives used to go up on their widow's walks to look for their husbands' ships sailing home. If they never *saw* their husbands' ships sailing home—well, I guess that's where the "widow" part comes in.

"Boy, what a view that balcony must have," I said.

"Really," Gabrielle agreed. "Hey—that gives me an idea! Wouldn't you guys like to watch the filming from up there? You'd be able to see everything that way."

"Do you think they'd let us?" I asked. "It would be great, but I wouldn't want to cause any trouble."

"I don't see how you'd be causing trouble," Gabby answered. "Some people might even think it was a good idea for you to be out of the way." She gave a dark look over at Caryl, who was earnestly going over her script with Reid. "That dopey Caryl has been complaining about you again, Meg. You've really gotten on her bad side somehow. Boy, she's sensitive—if that's not too nice a word for it."

"Then I'd *love* to be up on the widow's walk," I said quickly. "I don't want to be in the way."

"Can I stay on the ground?" asked Brooke. "Caryl's not mad at me—not yet, anyhow. And I don't like heights. I'd rather be down here where gravity can't get at me."

Gabrielle smiled. "Sure. Let me just go check with Kilmer that it's okay for you to be on the balcony, Meg."

The scene they were shooting was one in which Vincent came to Meg's house for the first time. While Brooke and I were grabbing some breakfast (there were about five thousand boxes of doughnuts on the set), Gabrielle went off to check with Kilmer about my watching the scene from the widow's walk.

"Sorry it took me so long," Gabrielle reported when she returned. "Kilmer was on the phone. But she says it's fine for you to watch from the widow's walk."

So I walked up through the old house. Up the wide marble staircase, past bedrooms with fireplaces and canopy beds, up to a slope-ceilinged third floor with a door that led out to the widow's walk. High above the ground, in the clear morning air, I stationed myself above the cameras to see what filming a movie scene looked like.

At first being up so high made me nervous. Also, I had to stand so still on that narrow balcony that I got cold. But watching the scene was interesting anyway.

I can report that someone really did shout "Places, everyone!" And someone else really did shout "Action!" And Kilmer really did shout "Cut!" when something went wrong, which happened a lot.

For instance, it happened when Meg was supposed to throw some mustard seeds at Vincent and Gabrielle threw the seeds into Mortimer's eyes by mistake.

"Ow, ow, ow!" yowled Mortimer. He dropped to the ground and started writhing around dramatically. "She's poisoned me! She's poisoned my *eyes!* I'm going to sue!"

"Cut!" came Kilmer's voice. "Makeup, please come wash out Mortimer's eyes. Try not to mess up his face."

The woman who'd done Mortimer's makeup earlier scuttled out and dabbed at his squinchedup eyes with a damp cloth. He struck out blindly at her.

"Don't touch me!" he yelped. "You'll make me even blinder!"

Gabrielle looked up at the widow's walk and rolled her eyes at me.

It seemed like hours before they got started again, partly because Mortimer wriggled so much that he smeared his makeup all over his collar and *did* have to be made up again.

A lot of things went wrong after that. Caryl hiccuped in the middle of one of her lines—she tried to pretend she'd done it on purpose as part of her "interpretation," but I didn't believe her. A seagull suddenly decided to fly through the scene. Someone noticed that Gabrielle's hair was parted on the wrong side. Except for the fact that the cameras were running, the whole thing just looked like another rehearsal. After about forty takes I started wishing I had brought a book with me. Or stayed on the ground, where I could at least have tiptoed away. I was afraid I'd make too much noise if I tried to leave the balcony now.

Bored, I leaned on the railing and stared out to sea. Far off on the horizon I could see a ship crawling slowly along; close by I could see the waves tracing lacy patterns on the shore. That was it for the sea.

More bored, I decided to take a little tour around the widow's walk. I tiptoed around one corner and stared down at some bushes. I tiptoed around the next corner and stared down at the house's back garden. I tiptoed around the third corner and stared at a slightly different view of the sea. I tiptoed around the last corner and, sighing, returned to my original spot. Maybe they were almost done with the scene *now!* I leaned over to check.

The railing quivered under my hand.

Quickly I pulled back—and wrenched the railing from its mooring as I moved.

Gasping, I pressed myself back against the wall. My heart was pounding.

The railing creaked, then began to buckle outward. And to my horror I saw that four of the posts holding it up were cracked.

Trying to grip the wall, I edged myself sideways. *The door, the door,* I was thinking frantically. I couldn't stay up here any longer. Suddenly the balcony seemed terribly narrow and tippy. Suddenly I began to imagine that the floor was shifting under my feet. Suddenly I was sure that if I took a step forward, I'd plunge through the gap in the railing. I had to find the door back downstairs.

Slowly, very slowly, I patted my way along the wall until I felt the edge of the doorjamb. Oh, thank heaven. I was safe now. A few more careful pats, and there was the doorknob. I took hold of it with trembling fingers and—

And it wouldn't turn. The door was locked behind me.

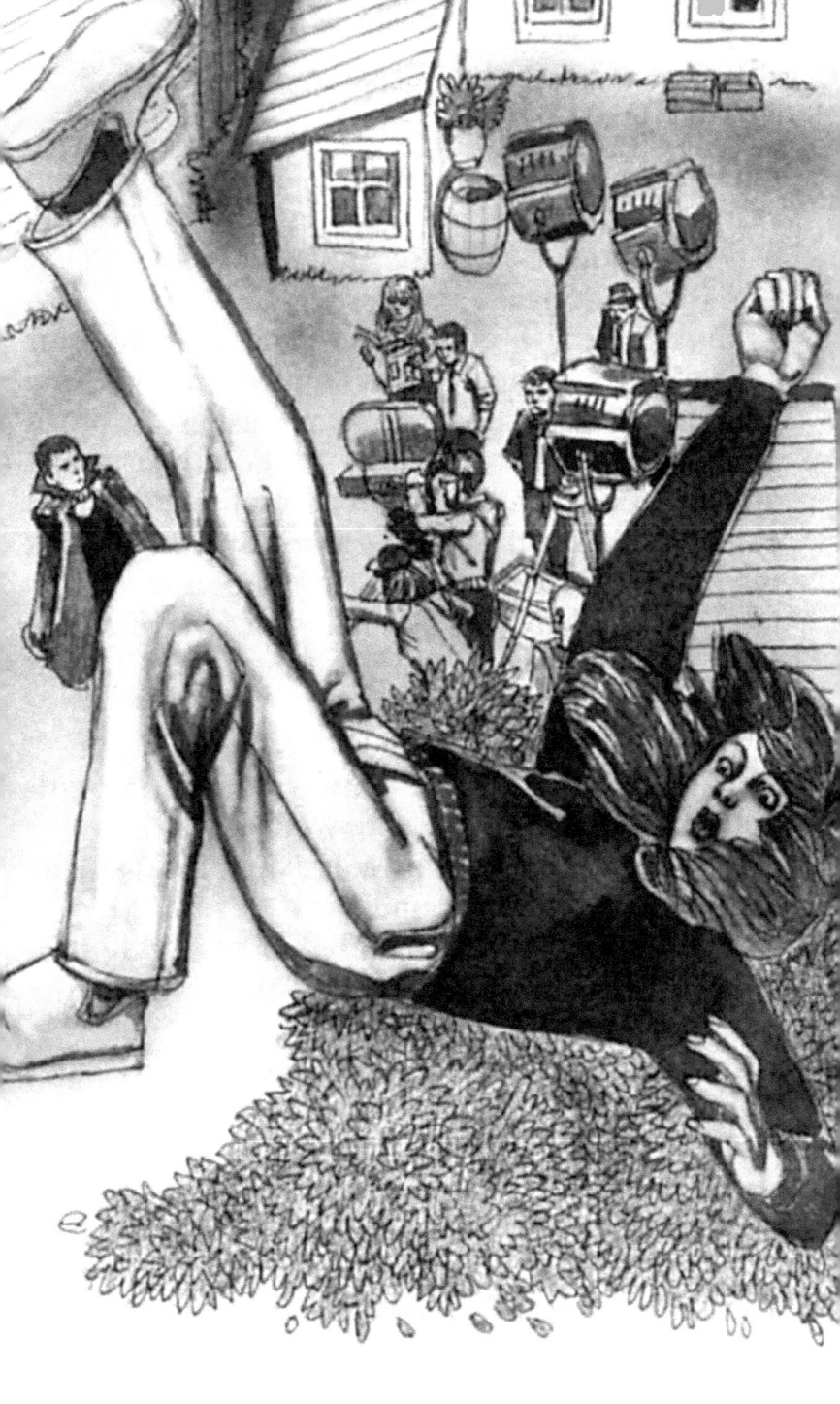

Locked! It couldn't be! I tried the knob again. Still it refused to move.

"This isn't happening," I whispered. I was starting to panic. I glanced back at the railing, and the sky tipped dizzily before my eyes. Was the floor really shifting under my feet, or was it just that I felt faint? What if the floor *was* shifting? What if it gave way?

I had to get out of there. Panicked now, I wrenched the doorknob with all my strength.

It ripped off in my hand.

With a shriek of terror I hurled backward through the gap in the railing and plunged toward the ground.

Chapter Five

The scream that had been tearing out of me stopped abruptly when I landed.

I didn't actually hit the ground. If I had, I probably wouldn't be telling you about this now. I fell in some bushes instead—the ones I had just been looking down on. This was good in terms of saving my life, but it was bad in terms of being more embarrassing.

In fact, as I gathered myself up and saw everyone shouting and rushing toward me, I wondered if it might have been better if I *had* hit the ground.

Brooke got there first. "Are you okay, Meg?" she gasped.

"I guess so," I said shakily. I could already feel a big bruise starting to throb on my forehead. My face was all scraped up, and my nose was bleeding. My ankle felt wrenched and sore, but I could stand on it okay.

"What *happened?*" asked Brooke, handing me a tissue.

Holding my head back, I dabbed at my nose. "The railing came loose, and when I tried to—"

"This is terrible," wailed Mortimer. "She could have fallen on me!"

"Or on me," added Caryl sharply. "I was even closer to her, actually."

"*Cut!*" Kilmer interrupted. She turned to the crew behind her. "Someone call an ambulance!"

Suddenly I remembered that the cameras had been running all this time. My spill into the bushes was now recorded on film.

"I—I really don't need an ambulance, Kilmer. I'm fine."

"You look terrible," Kilmer pointed out.

"Well, I'm a little bashed up. But mostly I'm just sorry to have caused trouble."

"I'm sure you are," said Kilmer coldly.

"I am! I didn't mean to cause trouble. Did I . . . wreck everything?"

Kilmer took a deep breath. She looked as if she was fighting to keep calm.

"You didn't wreck everything, no," she said tightly. "And of course I understand it was just an accident, and I'm glad you're not hurt, and all that. But let's just say it wasn't the most convenient timing. The scene was finally going well, and you—" She shook her head. "What on earth were you doing up there, anyway? This is a very old house! Things like that balcony are bound to be a little shaky."

"But you said it was okay for me to go up there," I protested. "Gabrielle told me so!"

Kilmer's eyes widened. "I said nothing of the kind. Gabby, what's going on?"

"Don't you remember?" whispered a wide-eyed Gabrielle. "You were on the phone. I asked if I could interrupt you for a second, and *then* I asked if it was okay. I can't believe you don't remember!"

There was a peculiar expression on Kilmer's face. "I don't think I'd forget something like that," she said slowly.

"It was probably an important call," Caryl butted in. "Naturally you have more on your mind than whether some kid gets to go up on a balcony. It wouldn't even have mattered if Meg hadn't been so clumsy."

"The door was locked," I protested, and explained how tugging on the knob had started my fall.

Kilmer took a deep breath. I could see that she was fighting to keep her temper.

"I'll have someone check the door and the railing," she said. "In the meantime, whatever happened, we're going to have to start over. Certainly the main thing is that Meg's all right. But, Meg, you do seem to have an unfortunate talent for getting in the way. Why don't you go and . . . calm down somewhere?"

She *still* sounded as though the whole thing had been my fault!

"The railing broke. I didn't break it," I said hotly. "I'm sorry I disturbed the scene, but it wasn't my fault."

Kilmer was silent for a minute, staring at me. Staring me down, it seemed. Finally she shook back her hair and turned away. "We won't discuss it anymore," she said crisply. "Let's take a break, everyone. We'll start shooting again in ten minutes."

Even her back looked angry as she walked off.

My legs were shaking, and I felt as though the whole world were staring at me. "Let's get out of here," I whispered to Brooke. As the cast and crew drifted away, Brooke and I began walking toward the beach.

Gabrielle was right behind us. "Wait a sec," she called in a low voice. When she caught up, I could see that she was trembling.

"I'm sorry. I'm sorry, Meg," she said. "I feel terrible about this."

"It's okay," I muttered. "You had nothing to do with it. Things just got mixed up."

"But that's the weird thing! They didn't get mixed up!" whispered Gabby. "I mean, Kilmer knew what she was saying. She *was* paying attention. She put the phone down to talk to me. She said there was a wonderful view from up there and that it was fine with her if you went up. I don't know how she could have forgotten that!"

She darted a look over her shoulder. "I'd better not let her see me talking to you," she said. "Something's definitely weird about Kilmer today."

Brooke and I watched in silence as Gabrielle dashed away. Then Brooke turned to me with a worried look in her eyes.

"Meg, did you lock the door when you got out onto the railing?" she asked.

"Of course not. Why would I have? I didn't even know it had a lock. Come to think of it, I don't even remember closing it behind me. I was trying so hard to be quiet."

"But, Meg, if you didn't lock the door . . . well, who did?"

"I don't know," I said slowly. "Maybe it blew shut and locked itself."

"It's not windy," Brooke pointed out. "And wouldn't you have heard a door slamming?"

"Yeah. Probably. But what are you getting at, Brooke?"

"I'm not sure I'm getting at anything," Brooke replied. "I just think it's weird that the door got locked and the railing broke at the same time. You could have really been hurt, you know."

"You mean you think someone might have locked the door on purpose? But why would anyone do that?"

Brooke shook her head. "I don't know. I guess they wouldn't. I'm probably imagining things."

I smiled ruefully. "It's nice of you to play detective, but I don't think I have any enemies here. Well, Mortimer. And Caryl. And Kilmer, maybe. I wonder why she—"

I stopped. All this time we'd been walking along the beach. Though it was only late morning, the sun seemed to have disappeared. The wind had a chilly edge, and the white-edged waves were a sullen gray.

"Let's go back," I said with a shiver. "Maybe we can get Dad to take us home. I don't feel like watching any more of the filming. In fact, I don't care if I never—"

I stopped in my tracks. Farther down the beach a little figure dressed in black was scampering along the sand. I couldn't see his face, but still I recognized him instantly.

"If you never what?" asked Brooke.

"Gribev," I whispered.

"If you never *gribev!* What are you talking about?"

"Do you see him?" I pointed a shaking hand.

"That little boy? Yes, I see him," Brooke said patiently. "What *about* him?"

"It's Gribev! I've got to catch up to him!"

I tore off down the beach as fast as I could.

"Who's Gribev?" I heard Brooke calling plaintively from behind me. "Meg, wait up!"

But I couldn't stop.

It was like chasing someone in a dream. I never seemed to get any closer. Once, the child turned and looked straight at me. Yes, it was exactly the same face I remembered—white and pointed, with black hair and huge dark eyes. He waved, then beckoned me on. His footsteps were etched sharp and clear in the sand.

Now he waved again and rounded a curve in the shore.

When I finally rounded the curve myself, I was too late. A tiny bat was already winging itself into the sky, flapping wildly and inexpertly.

I even recognized the way it flew.

"Gribev, come back!" I called frantically. "What are you doing here?"

A passing seagull screamed at me, but that was the only answer I got. The bat had already flapped itself out of sight.

Brooke caught up to me, out of breath.

"Meg, are you crazy? Who are you talking to? What's going on?"

"That was Gribev. And Gribev," I said shakily, "is Vincent Graver's little brother."

Brooke's eyes widened. "Vincent? Vincent the *vampire?*"

I nodded.

"The one who's been following you around for so long?"

"That's right. Every time I think he's gone for good, he turns up again. And every time he turns up again, it means something bad is going to happen." Which I guess isn't that surprising. You'd *expect* bad things to happen if a vampire was following you around.

"But . . . I thought Vincent was in Drazylvonia now." Brooke sounded completely lost, and I couldn't blame her.

"That's right," I said. "I last saw him on Christmas vacation, when *I* was in Drazylvonia. That's where I met Gribev, too. I thought he was a bat—a baby bat—but he turned out to be Vincent's brother instead."

"Well," said Brooke tartly, "you certainly keep quiet about what happens to you on vacation. You could have *told* me about this."

"Oh, Brooke, please don't you get mad at me, too. I wasn't keeping it a secret. It just seemed too complicated, and I wanted to forget about it all, and I figured I'd tell you someday. . . ." My voice was starting to wobble. This had been an awful, awful day. I fumbled around in my jeans pocket for a tissue, but of course I couldn't find one.

At that moment the sea let out a furious roar. We looked up, startled, just in time to see a huge wave rising up out of the water. And I mean *huge*. Ten feet tall, maybe, and curling over evilly, as if it meant to sweep everything in its path out to sea.

"Run!" I yelled to Brooke—but there was no time to run. The wave crashed down on the shore, throwing up huge jets of foam. A waisthigh wall of water rushed up and smacked us so hard it knocked us both over.

Soaked and sputtering, we watched as the tide pulled the wave back off the beach. And that was all. The sea became its choppy, sullen self again. Little whitecaps reappeared on the water—but there was no sign of another wave.

Brooke and I stared at each other, amazed. Then, slowly, we stood up again. We were both drenched to the skin—is there *anything* wetter than wet jeans?—and plastered with sand and seaweed.

"Ugh!" Brooke shuddered as she began wringing out her hair. "We'd b-b-better get back right away. I'm freezing."

But I was staring down at the sand.

"Brooke," I whispered, pointing a trembling finger. "Look."

There was writing on the sand where there had been water only seconds before. Somehow, the wave had washed a message up onto the beach.

The letters looked as if they'd been made by a finger—or a claw.

MEG SWAIN:

A VAMPIRE IS PRESENT, AND VERY CLOSE TO YOU.

YOUR LIFE IS IN DANGER. THE VAMPIRE WILL NEVER REST UNTIL YOU ARE DEAD.

BEWARE!

With a hiss, a smaller wave swished up on shore and erased the message before our eyes.

Chapter Six

A vampire is present, and very close to you.

I stared at Brooke.

"I'm not the vampire," Brooke said quickly. "You do know that, don't you?"

I had to smile. Brooke had once been bitten by a vampire and had almost turned into a vampire herself. But that's another story I don't have time to get into now.

"I know it's not you, Brooke. Don't worry," I said.

"Who could have written this?" Brooke asked. "Do you think it was Vincent?"

I shrugged helplessly. "Could be. Maybe that's why I saw Gribev. Or it could be that someone was warning me *about* Vincent—warning me that's *he's* the vampire who's present and close to me. I'm not sure."

"What about the handwriting? Did you recognize it?"

I laughed. "Handwriting in sand all looks the same."

"Oh. Right." Brooke sighed. "Well, how are we going to find out who wrote it? And how are we going to find out who the vampire is?"

"And how are we going to save my life?" I asked, and suddenly I wasn't laughing.

As I lay in bed that night, I had a sudden flash of hope. *Maybe*, I thought, *whoever wrote that message got confused by the movie. Maybe he, or she—or Vincent, or it, or whatever—thinks that Mortimer is a real vampire. Maybe I'm not in any danger at all.*

This thought was comforting enough to get me to sleep that night. But the next morning I found out that my invisible messenger had been telling the truth.

We picked up Brooke on our way to the set.

"Have you thought any more about the message?" Brooke asked in a low voice when she climbed into the car seat next to me.

"Duh! What do you think?" I hissed back. "It's practically *all* I've thought about."

"Me, too. And I've decided that Kilmer's the vampire."

"Kilmer? Why?" I asked.

"For one thing, remember her nickname? Kilmer the *Killer!* And she wears all that black, just the way vampires do. And that thing about giving Gabrielle permission to let you up on the widow's walk—I bet she's just pretending she didn't notice what she was saying. She probably wanted you to fall off."

"But why?"

"I don't know," Brooke admitted. "That part doesn't make much sense."

"She hasn't tried to bite me, either," I pointed out.

"Well, maybe she's going to! Maybe she's just waiting for the moment when she can—"

"What are you two buzzing about back there?" asked my father from the driver's seat.

"Oh, nothing," we said hastily.

"It's going to be fine, Meg," said my father. "No one's going to be mad at you for yesterday. You'll see." Obviously he didn't realize that that wasn't what we were talking about.

Still, Dad was right. When he dropped us off at the Fulton house, no one paid us a bit of attention. They were too busy wondering what had happened to Caryl, the woman who played "Meg's" mother in the movie.

Kilmer was standing on the front porch, yelling into a cellular phone. "She *has* to be at the hotel," she was saying. "She's not here, believe me. And we've been here for more than an hour. Call her room again, okay?"

A pause. Then Kilmer snapped, "All right, I heard you! She's not there!" She slammed down her cellular phone and stomped off the porch.

"Gabrielle!" she yelled in the general direction of the beach. "Hey, Gabby! Any luck?"

A couple of seconds later Gabrielle dashed up to us. "No. Sorry," she said, panting and flushed. "She's not on the beach. I looked everywhere."

Then Kilmer said something that would get me in trouble if I repeated it. "Everybody go away for a second while I think about what to do," she ordered.

People didn't just *go* away. They *tiptoed* away. Kilmer looked so mad that I guess no one wanted to make any extra noise.

"Caryl's late," Gabrielle whispered when she reached me and Brooke. We were standing off at one corner of the porch. I wished Dad were around—he could have taken us home. Or at least we could have gone and sat in the car until all the fuss was over.

"What scene were they going to shoot?" I asked.

"It's supposed to be the scene where Meg's parents have this private talk about Vincent because they're starting to worry that there's something the matter with him," said Gabrielle. (In real life my own parents never noticed that there was something the matter with Vincent. They probably wouldn't have noticed he was a vampire unless he'd walked up and bitten them on the neck.)

"It's a long scene, so Caryl would love it. Lots of lines and close-ups. It's not like her to be late," Gabrielle went on. "She loves hogging all the attention. I hope she's okay."

But Caryl *wasn't* okay.

Half an hour later, while Kilmer was making her jillionth phone call to one of the producers, Caryl came stumbling up the front walk of the house.

Kilmer dropped the phone and rushed up to her. "Where on earth have you been, Caryl?" she demanded. Then she stopped short and looked more closely. "Wait a minute. What's happened to you?"

Caryl's skin was grayish-white, and her eyes were dazed. She was pressing one hand against her neck as though it hurt. She turned slowly toward Kilmer and stared at her with polite interest, but she didn't answer.

"Are you sick?" Kilmer asked.

"Sick?" Caryl repeated in a strange, distant voice.

"Oh, cut it out," said Kilmer. "This is no time to try out a new interpretation. You're incredibly late, and—"

Suddenly Caryl began to speak. "I'm . . . not . . . sick. I . . . feel . . . very . . . well . . . thank . . . you," she said dreamily.

"I mean it, Caryl. I don't like this routine," Kilmer said. "Where were you, anyway?"

"I got a . . . message." Caryl moaned. "To go to . . ." She stopped, frowning. "I don't remember."

"Who gave you the message?" asked Kilmer.

"A person," said Caryl. Then she rubbed her neck fretfully. "It hurts," she whimpered.

Brooke gave me a frightened glance.

"Your neck hurts?" asked Kilmer. "Hey, there really is something the matter, isn't there?"

She took a step toward Caryl—and Caryl lurched backward with a cry of fear.

"Don't come near me!" she said. Both hands were clutching her neck now. "Get away!"

"I was just going to see if you have a fever," said Kilmer in surprise.

"Don't touch me!" Caryl wailed. She was starting to tremble now. "Why? Why is this happening? What did I do?"

A few interested bystanders had gathered behind her now. "Is she acting, or what?" I heard one of them ask.

Suddenly Caryl seemed to pull herself together. She stood up very straight, her eyes staring fixedly ahead of her.

"I won't let it near me again. I swear I won't," she said—and crumpled up in a dead faint.

Two red puncture marks shone wetly on her neck.

As you might imagine, that pretty much disrupted things for the rest of the morning. One of the producers helped Caryl to a car, drove her to the hotel, and put her to bed. Everyone else just clustered around, trying to wring as much drama as possible out of what had happened. Brooke and I didn't know what to do with ourselves—Dad was still off writing at the hotel—so we stood around, too.

"She was so pale!" one man said. "Whatever she has, I hope it's not something we can catch!"

"I think it is," a woman answered gloomily. "I'm starting to feel weak myself."

"You know, I had a kind of feeling something was going to happen to her," put in another woman. "Last night at dinner she definitely wasn't herself. I had a premonition that this might happen."

Sure you did, I thought. It drives me crazy when people tell you about a premonition *after* a thing happens. It would be a lot easier to believe them if they'd do it before.

"Lyme disease, that's what it is," said someone else. "Two dots on the neck like that—that's a sigh of Lyme disease."

That sounded totally made up to me. Hadn't any of these people ever heard of *vampires!*

"Whatever the matter is, it's very unprofessional of Caryl," came a lofty voice from behind me. "I'm surprised Kilmer hasn't suggested replacing her. *I* would never let down a production the way Caryl did today."

The speaker was Mortimer, of course. He was wearing his homemade vampire outfit, not his movie costume, and he had done his own stupid makeup. It was caked on his face in greenish streaks. He swished his cape around pompously, staring at me to see what kind of impression he was making. The main impression he made, though, was of a windup toy bat.

"Let's take a walk," I said to Brooke. "There's not much point hanging around here."

"You're right," she agreed fervently.

"Hey!" said Mortimer sternly. "I'm talking to you!" But we were already walking away.

"Who does he think he is?" I muttered to Brooke. "Our babysitter?"

The Fulton house had beach on one side and a few acres of pine forest on the other. Since Brooke and I had had such an unsettling time at the beach the day before, we found ourselves heading toward the woods without having to ask each other where we wanted to go. I guess it should have occurred to us that going into the woods with a vampire on the loose might not be the greatest idea, but it didn't. As soon as we were safely sheltered by trees, I asked, "So what do *you* think's the matter with Caryl?"

"Same thing you do," Brooke replied without quite meeting my eyes. "Mr. Vampire is back in town."

"Don't call Vincent 'Mr. Vampire'!" I protested. "He's not some cartoon character."

"Sorry. I was just trying not to sound scared. Whistling in the dark, I think they call it. You think it's a vampire, too, don't you?"

Oh, yes. I thought it was a vampire. Whoever was lying in wait for me had found another victim first. Which didn't mean I was off the hook, vampirely-speaking. I mean, the vampire hadn't decided to pick on someone else instead of me. He was probably just hungry. He'd probably just wanted Caryl as a snack until he got to me. . . .

"Maybe you should start wearing garlic around your neck," Brooke was saying. "That wards off vampires, doesn't it?"

"It's supposed to," I said, kicking a pinecone along as I walked. "The trouble is, sometimes it wards off people, too. I remember once when I—"

I froze in my tracks.

"Do you hear that?" I whispered. "Someone's coming toward us."

Now we *both* froze in our tracks. Someone was walking slowly and steadily through the trees. Making straight for us.

He wasn't making any effort to walk quietly, and the old leaves left over from the winter were rustling under his feet.

"Who's there?" I called out.

No one replied, but the walking continued.

Step. Step. Step. It was much closer now. Brooke's mouth was open, and she was breathing rapidly. She looked as if she might throw up.

Which would probably have been a good way to ward off a stranger, come to think of it. But I hated seeing Brooke so frightened. I had to try to calm her down.

"Mortimer?" I called sternly. "You're not scaring us. Why don't you go on back to your trailer and fix your makeup?"

A tense, I'm-working-at-it smile crept onto Brooke's face. "And go work on your accent, too," she called. "You sound like a kid in a cereal commercial, not a vampire."

The steps stopped. Good. We were getting to him.

"I'm so scared, Brooke," I whimpered in a mock-terrified voice. "Don't you think we'd better go back? We don't want any *vampires* to—"

A streak of black flashed before my eyes. A huge black shape hurtled through the air toward me. And the next thing I knew, I was being grabbed by a tall, black-dressed figure whose pointed teeth were only inches from my throat.

Chapter Seven

"Mortimer, let go of me!" I shrieked. "You— you—you *piggy ape!*"

I was too angry to come up with a better insult. I was also too angry to control myself. I wrenched myself out of Mortimer's grip and socked him hard in the stomach. Then I kicked him in the shins. I was just about to land another kick when Mortimer spoke.

"This is hardly the welcome I would have expected, Meg," he said in a deep, slow, cold voice, brushing sand off his cape. "Especially when one considers that I have flown several thousand miles just to speak with you."

I stared up at him—and my leg froze in midkick.

"Vincent?" I quavered.

"Yes. It is I."

That stern, pale, dead face did not belong to Mortimer, either. This was no Halloweenish imitation of a vampire in a fake cape and streaky green makeup, but the real thing. This was a real vampire looming up over me with the ocean crashing dramatically in the background.

This was Vincent Graver. I had been too busy kicking him to notice.

Brooke looked as horrified as I felt. I wouldn't have blamed her if she had turned and run, but she didn't budge. I think that's because she was such a loyal friend, but it may also have been that she was shaking too hard to move.

"I mean no harm," Vincent said reassuringly.

"What?" I said, backing up slowly. "You *always* mean harm! You're a *vampire!*" I reminded him.

"But this time I come in peace," he answered. "I have brought my younger brother with me— and he is very fond of you, as you know."

"So that *was* Gribev I saw," I said.

Vincent grimaced. "Yes, it was indeed. I regret to say that Gribev is being difficult lately. I find it almost impossible to control him. When he heard that I was coming after you, I could not deter him from materializing. He wished to see you in person. Now he is hiding, the little rascal. I shall probably have to hunt along miles of beach before he will reveal himself."

"Why have you—uh—come after me, anyway? Are you going to kill me?" I heard myself asking.

Vincent looked puzzled. "Kill you, Meg? What an odd notion. Do you not recall that we are no longer enemies? I have come to return your scarf, merely. You lent it to my brother back in Drazylvonia, and I wished you to have it back."

For a moment I totally forgot to be scared. "You came all the way from Drazylvonia to bring back a *scarf?*"

"I had business in the United States, also," Vincent admitted. "On the West Coast."

"What kind of business?" I couldn't help asking.

"Vampire business. A meeting of various vampire leaders from around the world."

"A meeting?" I echoed. "What on earth do vampires have meetings about?"

"This was a meeting about many things, including a stolen vampire treasure. It does not concern you," answered Vincent. "With my brother I took an airplane from California."

"Why didn't you just fly in your bat forms?" I asked. "I'm just wondering."

"We had *luggage,* Meg," Vincent said patiently. "Upon arrival in Delaware, we rented a car so that I could drive to you here. We so often meet at the seaside, do we not?"

I didn't care about that. "Go back to what you said before. You mean you have vampire *meetings?* You guys really get together to talk business? And rent cars?"

Vincent drew himself up. "The twenty-first century is almost upon us, Meg," he said huffily. "Vampires must learn to change with the times, just like humans."

"That makes sense," said Brooke bravely.

Vincent seemed to notice her for the first time. "Ah, Brooke," he said. "Hello. You appear to be in much better health than when I last saw you. From a human standpoint, at least."

Brooke had been about to become a vampire the last time Vincent had seen her. He had saved her from that fate—the only nice thing he had ever done for me. Of course I'd had to do something for him in return. That's how I had ended up on vacation in Drazylvonia—and that's how Vincent had ended up with my scarf. I had thought that would be the last I'd ever see of him, but now here he was again. Could it be that Vincent had really stopped hating me?

As if he had read my mind, Vincent said, "I am extremely worried about you, Meg. Did you get my message?"

He sounded as if it was a message on my answering machine, but I immediately knew what he meant. "The one in the sand? I wondered if you'd sent that."

"Yes, of course I had," said Vincent. "I sent it as soon as I realized the danger you were in." He cleared his throat. "A vampire is stalking you, Meg."

I felt my palms starting to sweat. "That's what you said in the message. But how do you know?"

"I felt a presence the instant I arrived in the state of Delaware. There was a certain electricity in the air. Vampires are adept at sensing each other."

"Kind of like dogs, maybe," said Brooke thoughtfully.

Vincent raised his eyebrows. "Perhaps so. In any case, the closer I drove to find you, the more certain I became of the danger. I was quite worried," he added. "I went too fast and got a speeding ticket.

"There is a strong aura of vampiric rage surrounding this spot," Vincent went on. "If the vampire cannot be discovered, your death is certain."

"Oh, no!" wailed Brooke.

"Well, who is it?" I squeaked.

"I cannot yet tell," admitted Vincent. "The disguise is too skillful. And if we cannot penetrate this disguise, your death is certain."

"Stop *telling* me that!" I snapped irritably. "Didn't your mother ever tell you that if you can't say something nice, don't say anything at all?"

For a second Vincent stared up at three seagulls wheeling in the clouds overhead. "I am not sure it is within my power to say nice things," he said. "But I would like to help unravel this mystery if I could. I might, perhaps, remain nearby for the next few days to see what I can discover. As you know, I am one of the very few vampires who can be outside in the daylight as long as I am not in direct sun."

"I don't think there's any danger of direct sun around here," Brooke put in with a shiver.

"So perhaps I could be useful to you," Vincent went on.

"Maybe you could," I agreed. "But what if someone sees you?"

"I shall take the form of a bat," Vincent replied. "Thus disguised, I can keep out of sight."

"You *better* keep out of sight, then," I warned him. "If anyone sees a bat in the daytime, they'll think it has rabies and call the police."

"Thank you for the warning. I shall not permit anyone to see me. However, I must find some way to occupy my little brother for this period of time. It would be too difficult to watch him *and* the filming. Has either of you any suggestions as to what I might do with Gribev?"

"You could find a day-care center for him, maybe," I suggested hesitantly. "There must be one in town."

"Day care? That is a form of technology with which I am not familiar. What does it do?"

"It doesn't *do* anything. It's sort of like nursery school," I said. Quickly Brooke and I explained what day care was. When we'd finished, Vincent looked relieved.

"This would be ideal for Gribev. Since he will never be a functioning vampire, it is good for him to meet normal human children."

There was something "wrong" with Gribev, I had learned in Drazylvonia. "Wrong" from a vampire point of view, that is. He wasn't dangerous or cruel, and he hated blood. To a vampire, this was considered a big problem. Without his "problem," though, I don't think Gribev would have been a very good day-care candidate.

"I shall now drive to town and find a day-care center," said Vincent. "Would you like to accompany me?"

"We can't," I said. "It'll be time for Dad to pick us up soon. He'd worry if we weren't here."

"Let it be so, then. Shall I meet you in the parking lot tomorrow morning?"

"Sure."

"Then I shall now take my departure."

He vanished, and high over our heads a bat zigzagged swiftly out of sight.

Chapter Eight

"I have located a day-care center for my brother," Vincent told me and Brooke the next morning. We had just arrived on the set—they were shooting on the beach today—and found Vincent lurking inside his rental car, waiting for us. We couldn't see much of him, though. The car had smoked-glass windows, and Vincent had only rolled down his window a few inches to talk to us.

"The center is called Wee Care Tiny Tykes." Vincent winced as he pronounced the name. "They appear to be most efficient. In fact, they asked me to provide a note from my parents stating that it was all right for me to pick up my brother in the car. I did not try to explain that I am several centuries old. . . .

"It seems a pleasant enough place, if you like pleasant places," Vincent went on. "I will not need to worry about Gribev while I am here. He will be taken care of until four o'clock each afternoon. And now, what about *us?* What is lying in wait for us today?"

"Nothing, I hope," I said with a laugh. "I think it's safe for you to come out. Everyone's down on the beach. Dad told me they're going to be shooting a swimming scene with Mortimer and Gabrielle."

Vincent frowned. "Is it warm enough for mortals to swim? I myself can withstand any temperature. But I would have said it was too early in the year for humans."

"Oh, I'm sure it's fine," I said.

And half an hour later, I was very excited to hear that I was going to be swimming in the scene.

"We need a kid for the beach scene," Kilmer explained. "Gabrielle's part calls for her to be on the beach the whole time, and we want someone to be swimming in the background."

"Great," I chirped. Lying, I added, "I love cold water."

"Well, I checked with the town health official," said Kilmer, "and he said that the water will be completely swimmable. Not the most comfortable thing in the world, but not dangerous, either. You won't freeze to death. Now, let's get going. There are a bunch of bathing suits in the trailer."

All the suits in the trailer looked straight out of Las Vegas. Fluorescent colors, ruffles, little gold belts, sequins, bows—they had everything I hate in a bathing suit. But I didn't care. I was going to be in a movie! Still, it took me a long time to find something that wasn't embarrassing.

Gabrielle, who was in the trailer having some last-minute makeup done, spoke up. "At least you get to be in the water most of the time. *I* have to spend the whole scene on the beach, trying to act as if I'm not totally freezing."

"Yes, but you're so tan," I said. "You'll look great no matter how cold you get." Even in a bikini, Gabrielle looked ruddy and comfortable.

"You don't want your necklace, do you, Gabby?" asked the makeup artist.

"Yes! Leave it alone!" said Gabrielle quickly. Now I noticed that she had a silver chain around her neck. A twisted silver charm, almost like a lightning bolt, hung from it. Gabrielle grabbed the charm as if she was trying to protect it. "I'm superstitious, remember? This necklace brings me luck. I've been wearing it for the whole shoot. Haven't you noticed?"

"But it was under your clothes before. Now it'll show up on camera," objected the makeup artist.

"I don't care," Gabrielle snapped. "If they don't want the actress wearing a necklace in this scene, they can find another actress."

"Hey, no problem," the makeup artist soothed her. "It was just a suggestion. Anyway, you're ready to go now."

There were about twenty other extras on the beach when we got there. Among them were a few little kids with pails and shovels, a couple of old people wrapped in beach robes, and several college-age kids who were supposed to be playing a volleyball game on the beach.

"I want you to drop your towel and run into the water," Kilmer told me. "Then start jumping around and playing in the waves."

"Okay, great," I said, my teeth chattering just a little as I gazed at the water.

"Good." She picked up her cordless phone and started barking orders into it.

Trying to look warm, I picked up my towel and headed slowly to the water's edge.

"I'll signal you when you're supposed to go in," Kilmer called after me. "Be watching for it. But don't *look* as if you're watching for it. Just act casual."

"Action!" she suddenly barked.

Instantly everyone on the beach looked busy and remote, as though they'd forgotten I existed. I stood there, jiggling from foot to foot and trying to look as if I wasn't watching Kilmer. I could see Gabrielle putting on sunscreen and leaning back luxuriously onto her towel under an imaginary sun. What an actress! She looked as if she were basking in ninety-five-degree air.

As soon as Gabrielle had settled down, Kilmer waved at me. Trying to look jaunty, I flung my towel onto the sand. Then I started running into the water.

Cold! The water was so totally *freezing* that for a second it jarred every thought out of my head. As soon as I was up to my waist, I dived under. Frantically I clawed my way upward to the air, which seemed almost balmy by comparison. But I couldn't let myself think about how cold I was. Arms churning, legs kicking, I started swimming.

Right away I got into trouble. A whirlpool sucked me under.

Down, down, down I swirled. *I'm not that far out,* I thought dazedly. *If I can just get my feet under me and stand up, I'll be okay.*

But the whirlpool was spiraling too hard for that. In its frenzied grip I flipped sideways, upside down, sideways again, like a smidgen of dust in a tornado. At the same time I could feel a terrible undertow pulling me farther out to sea. And I couldn't get my head above water.

I could feel my lungs hammering desperately, trying to force me to breathe. I knew I couldn't hold out much longer. In just a few seconds I'd inhale despite myself, and I'd be breathing icecold seawater. . . .

I've heard that when you're in the most danger, your body gathers strength from some unknown source. When I was sure my lungs were going to burst, I managed to grapple my way to the surface for just a second. I drank in a huge gulp of air, screamed "Help!" and then got sucked under the water again.

Dimly I remembered Kilmer's words. "You won't freeze to death," she had said. Too bad she hadn't promised I wouldn't drown. . . .

Chapter Nine

I'll never see Mom and Dad again. I'll never see Brooke, or my brother, I thought. Vincent's face flashed into my mind for an instant. Would he miss me?

Goodbye, Vincent. Goodbye, everyone.

I was dizzy now. Blue-white comets danced before my eyes. And then I heard a strange, throbbing hum.

It was coming closer, getting louder. Was I imagining it? Did people hear weird noises when they were about to pass out?

Suddenly I felt someone grabbing me from behind. A strong arm wrapped around my body. And before I had time to wonder what was happening, I'd been pulled to the surface.

"You're all right, Meg," I heard my father saying. "It's okay. It's okay."

The humming sound was a motorboat, I suddenly realized—and my father was sitting in it. My rescuer passed me up to him, and Dad pulled me quickly into the boat.

I hate to say it, but the first thing I did was throw up. Over the side of the boat, luckily. Then—even more embarrassingly—I burst into tears.

"You're okay, Meggie," Dad kept saying. But now I could see that his face was sickly pale. Despite the chilly air, sweat was rolling down his face.

He turned to my rescuer, who had clambered into the boat himself. "That was quick," he said in a shaky voice. "Thanks. I don't think I could've reached her fast enough if I'd just jumped in."

I recognized the man who'd pulled me up as one of the cameramen from the movie. He looked a little shaky, too.

"I can't understand what happened," he said. "That whirlpool ripped my motorboat right off its moorings. I reached it just in time," he said, slapping his arms to get warm. "Otherwise we might have had a bit of . . . trouble. Let's get back. Hey," he added suddenly, "look how calm the water is all of a sudden!"

He was right. The ocean was like glass—there wasn't a wave to be seen. If I hadn't been sopping wet, I wouldn't have believed I'd been in such danger just seconds before.

The cameraman started the motor with a roar, and in a few seconds we were pulling up onshore. Dad half-carried me out of the boat, then halfdragged me up to the beach. Brooke was waiting there with her blanket, which she flung over my head. I guess she was in too much of a hurry to aim straight.

"Oh, Meg, are you sure you didn't drown?" she asked frantically.

I pulled the blanket off my head. It looked as if everyone on the beach had surrounded me. "I think I didn't," I said, or rather coughed. "I'm still here."

"What happened, Meg?" It was Kilmer. I was glad to see that she looked worried, not mad.

"There was some kind of whirlpool thing out there," I told her. "As soon as I got over my head, it—it grabbed me." I shuddered.

"You shouldn't have started swimming. You should have kept your feet on the ground. You were just supposed

to be jumping around," Kilmer said reprovingly. (I guess she was a *little* mad.) "The undertow's a lot stronger than you'd expect. I thought your dad said you'd had experience in the ocean."

"I have!" I protested. "That whirlpool came out of nowhere."

"I'd better take you home," said Dad.

"No way, Dad! I'm fine!" I was *determined* not to cause any more trouble now. "Besides, don't you need to work? What are you doing here on the beach, anyway?"

"I just came here to see how your scene was going," Dad told me. "I got here just as people were noticing that you were in trouble, and—and here we are."

"Well, now you can get back to work," I said stoutly. "My clothes are in the trailer. All I have to do is change back into them, and I'll be fine." I turned to Kilmer. "If that's okay, I mean."

"It sure is," she answered. "I wouldn't dream of sending you back out into the water. You run on over to the trailer and get changed. I'll send someone over with a hot drink in a little while."

It was the nicest Kilmer had ever been to me. I flashed her a shivery smile and jogged stiffly off toward the trailer, still wrapped in the blanket. Brooke came along with me.

Inside the trailer it was nice and warm. But even when I'd finished changing, I couldn't stop shaking. Even after Brooke had dried my hair with a blow-dryer we found, I couldn't stop shaking. Even after I'd lain down on a cot in the corner and Brooke had covered me with blankets, I *still* couldn't stop shaking.

"You've got to stay here and get warm," Brooke told me at last. "I'll go and tell your dad where you are. And I'll come back in and check on you in a little while."

My teeth were chattering too hard for me to answer.

Brooke threw someone's coat on top of my pile of blankets, then slipped out of the trailer. After a few minutes I could feel myself slowly starting to thaw out.

A wonderful creamy warmth began to wash over me, and I relaxed at last. I must have drifted off to sleep, because the next thing I noticed was a little click at the trailer door. I opened my eyes halfway. Had Brooke come in to check on me? No, it was Gabrielle. But I was too tired to speak to her. My eyes closed again, and I buried my face in the pillow.

"Meg?" Gabrielle whispered. "Kilmer asked me to bring you some hot chocolate. Do you want it?"

"Nnnnnnnnn," I murmured. Even opening my mouth to answer was too hard.

"Meg?" Gabrielle said more loudly. "Meg, here's your hot chocolate from Kilmer." She crossed the floor toward the cot and shook my shoulder gently.

"I'm okay," I mumbled. "Just want to sleep. . . ."

"Kilmer said you should have this," Gabrielle insisted. "She'll be mad if I don't get you to try some. Just have a little bit, okay?"

I sighed and opened my eyes halfway. Gabrielle was staring down at me with a worried look on her face.

"Only a little," she said again. "Here, let me give you a hand."

She helped me sit up, then carefully guided the cup toward my mouth."

"Careful, now. Don't spill it."

The hot chocolate was delicious, and I drained the cup. Gabrielle looked much happier when I was done. "Do you think you can get back to sleep?"

"I *know* I can," I told her. "Thanks, Gabrielle."

I must have slept for a couple of hours. It wasn't until Dad and Brooke came looking for me that I finally woke up again.

"It's time we headed home, Meg," said Dad. "Can you make it out to the car?"

"Make it out to the car," I repeated slowly.

"That's right. I won't have to carry you, will I? Because you're getting so big that—"

"So big that," I interrupted. My voice seemed thicker, somehow. I tried it out again. "So big that. So *big that!*" My tongue didn't seem to be working right. I let out a silly giggle.

"Meg?" Dad looked concerned.

"I'm all right, Daddy. Daddy-oh," I added, giggling again.

My father reached out and felt my forehead.

"I think you have a fever, sweetie," he said. "I'm going to bring the car right up to the door. I'll be back in a second."

"A second, a second," I crooned to myself, in a little singsong. "Back-in-a-second. Back-in-asecond. Back-in-a—"

"Meg, what are you doing? What's the matter?" Brooke bent over me. She looked as if she was about to cry.

"What's the matter? What's the *matter!*" I repeated angrily. The words felt as though they were coming from someone else. "Can't you see what's the matter?"

"Whoops," said my father, who had just come back into the trailer. "She's delirious. We're going to the hospital, Meggie."

I don't remember much about the ride to the hospital, or about the hospital itself. Later, Brooke told me that all the other patients in the emergency room were quite interested in how crazily I was talking. I'm glad I don't remember *that*. In fact, the only thing I can recall clearly is the reddish beard of the intern who finally came in to examine me.

"She's been poisoned," he said immediately.

You don't really need to hear about how I had my stomach pumped out. It's not my favorite thing that ever happened to me, and I've done my best to forget the details. The only thing I remember clearly is Brooke leaning over my bed once she and Dad had taken me home and gotten me upstairs. Dad was downstairs looking for a hot-water bottle—with Mom and Trevor away in Disney World, he didn't know where anything was—and Brooke must have figured that this was the only chance she had to talk to me.

"Meg, can you hear me?" she said.

I felt too weak to answer, but I nodded.

"Meg, do you think it was the hot chocolate that did this to you?"

I nodded again. I had only the haziest memory of drinking the hot chocolate, but what else could have made me sick?

"Meg, Kilmer made that hot chocolate herself. I saw her."

I moved my head feebly to show that I was listening.

"She must have put something in it," Brooke went on intently. "Do you want me to call the police?"

"No proof," I said in a hoarse whisper.

"I know, but—"

My father came in before Brooke could say anything more.

"I couldn't find the hot-water bottle," he told us helplessly. "But I did find that old hot-tray Mom and I got for a wedding present. Do you think it would work if I wrapped it in a towel?"

I summoned up all my energy to answer him. "Right, Dad," I rasped. "I'm really going to be comfortable lying on a *tray*."

The effort of being sarcastic must have been too much for me, because I didn't hear his answer. I had fallen asleep.

Kilmer was stalking me, her face dark with fury and her eyes burning like coals. We were standing on the beach, and it was the middle of the night. A dagger glinted in the moonlight as Kilmer raised it to stab me. Terrified, I stepped backward toward the water.

"That's right," said Kilmer. "Keep going."

I cast a glance over my shoulder. The ocean was dark and menacing, and it was waiting for me.

Kilmer gestured with the dagger, and I took another step backward.

"Keep going," she repeated. "You know what you have to do. You know where you have to go.

"You know I need to get rid of you. Now move."

But I couldn't move. The terror of walking into that dark water—of feeling the cold waves closing over my head—was stronger even than the terror of Kilmer's dagger.

Silently I shook my head.

"You give me no choice," Kilmer said icily. She took another step forward. Her hand closed around my shoulder and began to shake me. . . .

"*Meg*. Wake up," came a low voice. "You are having a bad dream."

Dazed, I opened my eyes. A rush of relief spread over me as I realized I was lying in my own bed. Someone really *was* shaking my shoulder. I couldn't see who it was, though.

"Dad?" I whispered.

"No. It is not your father. It is I."

In the moonlight I could see his pointed teeth gleaming.

"Vincent!" I lurched backward in my bed and switched on my bedside lamp. "What are you doing here?"

"I came to make sure you were all right after the events of today. There was no way I could reach you during the daytime—you were never alone."

"Except for when I practically drowned," I said crossly. "If you're so interested in how I am *now*, why didn't you give me a hand *then*?"

"Did you not notice when the water became calm? That was my influence. There are certain spells . . . I can, on occasion, influence nature by the force of my concentration. I sensed that you were in danger and sent what aid I could."

"I guess you weren't concentrating very hard, then," I said crossly. "The water didn't calm down until I had already been rescued."

"These are foreign waters," Vincent explained. "Perhaps it took them longer to receive my message. Or perhaps—" He stopped, frowning. "I cannot swear to it, but it almost seemed that the other vampire was opposing my powers."

"How?" I asked blankly. "Can *all* vampires make water do weird stuff?"

Vincent shook his head. "No, indeed. The power of controlling nature belongs to very few of the most ancient families. Possibly I am mistaken."

So I went back to the reason he was in my room. "I don't want you checking on me in the middle of the night. You're not a comforting person!"

Besides, I didn't want Dad to hear me and Vincent talking. I couldn't *possibly* have convinced him that I was being delirious in two different voices.

"You have to go!" I whispered. "Thanks for helping me. Now, get out of here."

"Fine, if that is your wish," said Vincent coldly. "I have no need to stay where I am not wanted."

He was reaching into a pocket as he spoke. He pulled out some crumpled pieces of paper and tossed them at the foot of my bed.

"I almost forgot. My brother made these pictures for you in day care."

I picked up the pieces of paper and smoothed them out. Even though Gribev was a vampire, I could see that his drawing style was pretty much like any three-year-old's. True, he had drawn everything in black—but maybe that had been the only crayon left.

"Thanks," I said. "Tell Gribev thanks, too," I added more warmly.

Then I looked at Vincent more closely. "Vincent, you've got white stuff all over you."

"Paste," Vincent said gloomily. "The other projects Gribev brought back to our hotel were completely covered with paste. Now I am completely covered with paste. This makes it very difficult for me to fly."

I couldn't help chuckling. "I can imagine." We were silent for a moment. Then I said, "Vincent, I was dreaming about Kilmer when you got here. Do you think she's the other vampire on the set?"

Vincent shrugged carelessly. "It may be that she is. Someone on the set is very angry at you. Enraged, actually—enraged to the point of madness. Kilmer is perhaps the only member of the crew with a reason for this anger."

"I know." My voice was bleak. "I've messed things up a couple of times."

"Although Caryl also seems to hate you, as does Mortimer."

"That's true. They're both such idiots that it's hard to believe they could be vampires, though. Still, I'm starting to have a lot of enemies. Maybe I shouldn't go to the set anymore."

"You would be safer to stay at home, certainly. And yet I hope you will decide to continue. There is no way we can expose this other vampire without you, Meg."

"Why not?"

I have to confess, I was hoping that Vincent would say something about how smart I was, or how experienced at tracking down vampires, or something like that. But his answer was considerably less flattering.

"We need you as bait," he said.

Chapter Ten

"What is going on here!"

It was Kilmer's voice, and she was furious. But for once it wasn't at me.

It was Mortimer she was yelling at—a Mortimer I hadn't seen before. Brooke and I had just arrived on the set to find the cast and crew gathered around him. He was pale and shivering, his skin a sickly gray that didn't look like his usual amateurish makeup job. He was staggering a little, and wincing as if the light hurt his eyes.

"You were supposed to be in the trailer at six a.m.," Kilmer told him. "It is now *eight* a.m. Gabrielle's made up. We can't start the scene until you're all made up. *Where have you been!*"

"I . . . don't know," said Mortimer in a hollow voice.

"You don't *know!*" Kilmer repeated furiously.

Mortimer passed a hand across his throat. "Something happened," he said vaguely. "What was it?"

Brooke glanced at me. "Just like Caryl," she whispered. I nodded. It looked to me as though Mortimer had been attacked by a vampire, too.

Abruptly he dropped to his knees. He was still paler now. If he hadn't been Mortimer, I would have felt sorry for him.

Kilmer obviously wasn't worried about him, though. "Mortimer, I've had enough of your antics," she said crossly. "It's bad enough that you stay in character one hundred percent of the time. Now you have to start copying Caryl."

"Not . . . copying . . ." It was hard to hear Mortimer. He was now lying facedown on the ground.

"Get up, Mortimer," ordered Kilmer. "I can't take any more of this."

Mortimer didn't move.

He didn't move some more.

"Get up," Kilmer said again.

More nonmovement on Mortimer's part.

"Oh, for heaven's sake," Kilmer muttered. She leaned over and grabbed Mortimer's arm.

At once her expression changed. She slid her fingers down to his wrist. "His pulse is awfully low," she said, almost to herself. "And he's cold."

"He's dead!" someone behind me gasped hysterically.

"Of course he's not dead," Kilmer snapped in her ordinary voice. "He's only fainted or something." She rubbed her forehead in exasperated worry. "I swear, this set is cursed. Can someone call a doctor? Mortimer's out of commission. We'll have to film a different scene," she added over her shoulder to her assistant.

With those words Mortimer's natural vanity must have come back. "No doctor. Okay now," came his voice—seemingly from deep inside the ground.

As we watched, he slowly pushed himself to his feet. Still staggering, he took a couple of steps toward Kilmer.

"I'm a professional," he said in the ghost of his normal voice. "I c-can do the scene."

Kilmer stared at him. "Are you sure?"

"Sure."

"Okay, then," Kilmer said after a second. "Let's do it, gang."

Everyone started rushing around except for Mortimer, who stood where he was. No one seemed to be paying him much attention, so I walked over to him.

"Mortimer, what *did* happen?" I asked quietly. "Do you remember?"

Mortimer rubbed his throat again. "Something bit me," he said in a puzzled voice. "See?"

I certainly did. There were two puncture marks in his neck, just as there had been in Caryl's. I couldn't help being glad that at least two other people on this set were vampire bait besides me.

"But who did it?" asked Brooke.

"I'm not sure," said Mortimer. In a stronger voice he added, "I told you, I'm a . . . professional. I don't . . . pay attention to these things."

"Whatever happened to him, he's still as obnoxious as ever." It was Gabrielle, who had come up behind me without my noticing. "Come on. Let's leave him alone," she added, practically dragging us away.

"You can't leave me alone," Mortimer called after her. "I'm *in* this scene with you."

"Oh, yeah. That's right." Gabrielle slowed down. "I forgot."

"You forgot which scene we were doing?" Mortimer's voice was almost back to its normal level of pompousness. "It's *only* the most important one in the whole film."

"Oh, right," Gabrielle muttered. "The big fight scene."

"I prefer to think of it as the film's high point," said Mortimer grandly.

"You die in it, if that's what you mean," snapped Gabrielle.

"Temper, temper!" said Mortimer, who now (unfortunately, seemed almost fully recovered. He whooshed his cape around. "Shall we head for the cliff, ladies?"

The first summer I knew Vincent—the summer when he was my babysitter—is so long ago that it seems like a dream now. A nightmare, really. I can hardly believe that the nightmare happened to me. And the most nightmarish adventure of that whole summer was the time I tracked down the hut where Vincent slept in his coffin during the day.

"My" hut had been deep in the woods, but the one they were using for the movie looked even scarier. It was a ramshackle building with a crumbling chimney and a crooked, weed-edged front path. Behind the cliff the white-capped sea stretched out for miles. Above the sea the gray sky was filled with scudding clouds.

"Who could ever have lived here?" Brooke murmured, echoing my thoughts exactly. "It's so lonely!"

Gabrielle, who was walking a few steps ahead, turned around. "Actually, this hut was built for the movie. They did a good job, didn't they?"

"Too good," I muttered. I wondered if Vincent could see the hut from wherever he was hiding. I wondered if he remembered how he'd chased me when he had found me there. I wondered if he felt sorry about that now. At least Gabrielle didn't have to worry about any *real* vampires in there.

Mortimer's voice cut into all this wondering. He was striding back and forth along the cliff, waving his cloak and muttering to himself. Getting in character, probably.

"Gabrielle! Gabrielle, come over here," he called bossily. (Gabrielle had been peering through the windows of the hut.) "I want to go over a few things with you."

I could see Gabrielle sigh, but she trudged down toward us. "What is it *now*, Mortimer?" she asked when she reached us.

"You don't have to take that tone," Mortimer said loftily. "I just wanted to say that when I'm chasing you, you should try to look as small as you can. I'll look a lot scarier that way."

"Hey, great idea," said Gabrielle. I don't think Mortimer had any idea that she was being sarcastic. "Do you have any suggestions about how I can look small when I'm running along a cliff? Maybe I should burrow underground instead. That way you could run right on top of me."

"Oh, I don't think *that* will be necessary," Mortimer said seriously. "Just hunch down out of the way and the audience won't notice you too much."

This discussion was cut off by Kilmer's arrival. As usual, she was followed by a pack of camera people and assistants; as usual, she looked one hundred percent businesslike. If she *was* possibly a vampire—and I couldn't believe she was—she sure hid it well.

"Let's get going, guys," she called. "Mortimer, you go up and get into your coffin."

"Avec plaisir, mademoiselle," said Mortimer proudly. He swept her a low bow and began striding up the cliff.

Kilmer sighed. "And you, Gabby—we'll start with you discovering the hut."

Gabrielle nodded.

"Remember," Kilmer continued, "you're not *looking* for the hut in this scene. You're just wandering along. You find the hut by accident, and when you look inside you realize that this is where Vincent's been living all the time. That's when you start to get scared."

Gabrielle nodded again.

"Places, everyone," said Kilmer. "And . . . action!"

Gabrielle began walking. The top of the cliff was windy, and wind whipped her hair into a cloud of tangles as she wandered along. Wind grabbed the door of the little hut and began banging it violently back and forth. Wind tossed the seagulls through the air and churned the sea into such a mass of foam that you could hardly see the water at all.

It was perfect.

I could hardly believe that this was just a movie set. As I watched Gabrielle struggle along the cliff, I began to feel that she really *was* me, and my heart thudded with fear at the discovery she was about to make. In just a second she'd reach the hut and find out what was inside. . . .

Now she was there. For an instant she leaned against the hut to shelter herself from the wind. Then she felt her way along the wall until she reached the hut's tiny window.

Vincent is inside, I found myself thinking. *Does he know she's coming! Is he waiting for her!*

Oh, what was going to happen?

Gabrielle peered inside the hut. Her eyes widened with fear. She opened her mouth to scream.

Then, suddenly, she turned around. "Can we do another take?" she called to Kilmer, who was standing a little way down from the hut.

"Cut!" Kilmer called. "What's the matter "

"I—I can't quite feel the mood," Gabrielle confessed. "I'm really sorry."

Kilmer looked baffled. "I thought you were great," she said. "But sure, we can do it again."

This time, though, the wind died down just as Gabrielle started her walk toward the hut. And even I could see that the mood of the scene was flat. Instead of wandering toward her doom, Gabrielle just looked as if she was plodding along thinking about her homework.

"Cut!" Kilmer called again. Then, patiently, "Gabby, that was a little tame. Let's try it one more time."

And one more, and one more, and one more after that. Something kept on going wrong—and more often than not, the "something" was Gabrielle. I had never seen her so nervous. Once she got through the whole scene, but then banged into the door of the hut when Mortimer (playing Vincent) began to chase her. Once she got the giggles when she was supposed to look terrified. Several times she just quit in the middle for no reason that any of us could see.

The day dribbled slowly on.

"I don't know what's the matter with me," Gabrielle confessed during a break as she, Brooke, and I huddled in the picnic shelter. "I'm not usually like this."

"Because you're not really a professional," put in Mortimer haughtily. He was getting into the lunch line for the third time. "I hope Kilmer learns her lesson this time. It never pays to work with amateurs."

Gabrielle's eyes filled with tears. "Maybe that *is* the problem," she choked out. "Maybe I just wasn't meant to be an actress."

"Mortimer!" snapped Kilmer. "Don't be like that. You've had your share of off days, too." To Gabrielle she added, more gently, "It'll go better this afternoon."

Unfortunately, it didn't work out that way. The afternoon went even worse than the morning. After Gabrielle had made about a thousand mistakes, Kilmer called a halt.

"We might as well stop for today," she said. "It's four o'clock."

That meant Vincent would be leaving to pick up Gribev from day care. I wondered if he'd been bored watching this all day.

"It's supposed to rain soon, and we're all tired," Kilmer continued. "Besides, I've got to listen to a tape of the score for one of the scenes now. The conductor has to fly to L.A. tonight. She stopped by the set on her way to the airport. We'll try again tomorrow, okay?"

As the cast and crew started to drift away, Gabrielle walked over to me and Brooke.

"Well, I've totally mined a day of shooting," she said mournfully. "Listen, guys—I'm getting desperate here. Could you possibly rehearse the scene with me, Meg? You can use my script and read Vincent's lines. I *can't* let this happen again tomorrow!"

I checked my watch. "I'd be happy to, but I'll have to call the hotel and check with my dad. He may want to go home pretty soon."

"Let him go, you fool!" said Gabrielle.

" *What!*"

"I—I—" Gabrielle rubbed her eyes. "I'm sorry. I don't know why I said that. Mortimer must be rubbing off on me. What I meant to say was, why don't you just let your dad go home? There's a car service in town. I can call them when we're done and have them take you home after they drop me off."

"I'll go home with your dad, Meg," offered Brooke. "Then you guys can start working right away."

"Oh, would you?" said Gabrielle gratefully. "That would be so nice. Here, Meg. Here's a script."

At that moment a thunderous burst of music blasted the air. We all jumped. Then Gabrielle laughed.

"Kilmer must be listening to the score," she said. "She likes her music *loud*. At least it'll give us some atmosphere."

As Brooke trotted off to call the hotel, Gabrielle gave me my instructions.

"You wait inside the hut until I come in," she said, forgetting that I had watched the scene about fifty times already. "You don't really have to lie in the coffin, of course."

That was a relief.

"But I'd prefer it if you would," Gabrielle went on. "It would get me more in the mood for really killing you. So then I say my Meg lines, and you say your Vincent lines, and you chase me out of the hut, and we have our big scene on the cliff," Gabrielle went on. "And then I kill you."

There was a pause.

"I pretend to, I mean," said Gabrielle. "Shall we get started?"

The music wound eerily through the air, blending with the wind as I made my way into the hut. It was pitch dark in there, and the coffin was just a darker patch on the dark floor. I knew it wasn't a real coffin, but I didn't like being in there with it. *I don't really have to get into the coffin,* I told myself. *Gabrielle won't care.* I edged myself as close to the door as possible and waited for Gabrielle.

In a couple of minutes she was staring through the window of the hut. Cautious and wide-eyed, she walked inside—and then she frowned at me.

"Why aren't you in the coffin, Meg? I *said* I wanted you in the *coffin!*"

"Okay, okay," I said, startled. "I didn't think it mattered that much."

Gabrielle spoke through clenched teeth. "I just want to get this over with, okay? Let's start again."

This was beginning to be not as much fun. *Oh, well,* I thought, *she's just nervous.* Wincing a little, I lay down in the coffin and waited for Gabrielle to start the scene again.

"Good. That's a lot better," she said when she saw me in the coffin. "Now just close your eyes for a minute, so I can get in the mood."

Somehow I didn't like the sound of that, but I closed my eyes. There was a little silence. I could hear the wind moaning outside. Then Gabrielle said, "Okay, you can open your eyes again. So now I say bla bla bla—I know those lines, I don't have to rehearse them—and you chase me out to the cliff," she directed me.

The wind was blowing fiercely as I raced out of the hut after her. It almost knocked me over. All around me the tall grass was shivering, and I could see the sea pounding below the cliff. To top things off, it was starting to rain. I wished I had brought something warmer than my denim jacket with me.

"Okay. Here's where we stop," Gabrielle said tensely. She pointed to a little ledge that jutted out farther than the rest of the cliff. I reached for my script, but she shook her head.

"You really don't need to read. I know this part by heart. Just grab me by the shoulders as if you're going to push me over the cliff."

I took her shoulders gingerly. "I'll be careful," I promised.

Gabrielle gave an odd little laugh. "Oh, you don't need to be careful, either. I know this part by heart," she repeated. She was staring at me intently as raindrops streamed down her face.

"Okay. Now we have to pretend to fight a little," she said, and laughed again. Gripping my shoulders painfully, she began to shake me— hard. I could feel my feet actually leaving the ground.

"Wait a sec," I objected. "That's too much!"

"Oops. Sorry," Gabrielle said breathlessly. "Here—let me—"

And suddenly she kicked my ankle—so hard that I pitched forward. For a second, I actually teetered over the edge of the cliff.

The sea seemed to sway beneath me.

"Stop it! What are you doing?" I cried, alarmed.

"I'm pushing you over," said Gabrielle. And slowly, with one foot twisted around my ankle, she began to push my shoulders.

"That's not funny." I was having a hard time breathing. "I really don't like this, Gabrielle."

"Good," she rasped in a voice I'd never heard before. "You're not supposed to like it." She was still gripping my shoulders, but now she had me almost parallel to the sea below. She loosened her hold for a second, then yanked me up abruptly. "How does *that* feel?" she rasped again.

Horrified, I twisted my head to look up at her.

Then I screamed.

Gabrielle's ruddy face was drenched with rain now. At first I thought that patches of her skin had washed away. Then I realized that the water had taken off makeup, not skin. And under the makeup, her face was a sickly greenish-white. Surely no living human's skin had ever been that color. The only time I had ever seen such a face had been on a—

"Vampire," I whispered. "You're a vampire."

"What else could I be?" Gabrielle asked.

Her eyes were blazing with hatred, her face was contorted into a snarl—revealing long, sharp teeth.

I screamed again, but the wind and the rain and the eerie music swallowed the scream before it could go anywhere.

"I've been waiting for this, Meg," said Gabrielle. "At last my r-r-r-revenge is at hand."

Now, underneath the rasp in her voice, I could hear the foreign accent that had never been there before.

She bent her face close to mine.

"See *how it feels to die!*" she shrieked.

Chapter Eleven

"Why are you doing this, Gabrielle?" I screamed. Maybe it wasn't the most original thing to say, but under the circumstances I thought I should know.

For a split second she yanked me back up, twisting my face toward hers.

"There are two reasons. First, Vincenzio was mine," she growled. *"Mine.* Five centuries before he knew you, he was mine. I will see you rot before you ever lay a hand on him again."

I stared at her blankly, appalled. "You—you're insane," I finally whispered. "I have absolutely no idea what you're talking about."

"How well she lies," Gabrielle muttered. And she kicked me over the cliff like a thrown-out doll.

You hear about people's lives flashing before their eyes when they're about to die, but I felt nothing like that. All I could think was that Brooke wouldn't know where to find me. I'd be lying dead at the bottom of the cliff, and she'd never know what had happened. . . .

I hit the ground sooner than I had expected to. A *lot* sooner. In fact, I hit the ground almost immediately.

Well, not the ground, exactly. Perhaps ten feet below the lip of the cliff, a safety net jutted out. *Of course!* I thought joyfully as I bounced gently into the net's embrace. *They couldn't have filmed a fight on a cliff without something like this!* I lay there for perhaps a second. Then, almost before I realized what had happened, I had jumped to my feet and begun clambering up the cliffside like a panicked squirrel. My sudden release made the climb seem like nothing at all— until I was almost at the top of the cliff.

"Try nothing," came the hateful voice above me. "True, I forgot the net was there. But that does not mean you are saved. The instant your wretched hands come scrabbling up here, I shall kick them down again."

I guess it was too much to expect that Gabrielle would have gone away without checking to see what had happened to me.

She was leaning over the cliff and calmly watching my approach as if I were a beetle she was waiting to crush. She looked even more ghastly now. Rain had washed away the last vestige of her makeup, and her skin was the color of a frog's stomach. Her drenched hair was wrapped around her like a tom black sheet, and her eyes looked as flat and evil as a reptile's.

I'm not known for my brilliant one-liners. In a detective story this would have been the place where I would have made Gabrielle confess everything. Instead, I blurted out, "Why don't you just suck my blood instead of going to all this trouble?"

Gabrielle laughed scornfully. "I do not want your vile blood mingling with mine," she said. "Nothing would be more sickening to me. To feast on the blood of the brat who stole my Vincenzio—*faugh!* The very thought makes me ill."

Sudden fury drove away my fear for an instant. "Gabrielle!" I shouted. "Will you please tell me *what you're talking about!* If you're going to kill me, I have a right to under-stand what's going on. *Who's Vincenzio!*"

"*I* am Vincenzio," came a voice from behind Gabrielle. And Vincent's head loomed up over hers.

"Vincent?" I asked, in almost my normal voice.

But he didn't answer me. Gabrielle had whipped around to face him, and the two of them were staring at each oth-er. I froze at the cliff's edge, balancing precariously on a root and hanging on with my fingertips.

"So," Gabrielle said with deadly hatred. "We meet again."

"We do, indeed," said Vincent, equally coldly. "A most unwelcome occurrence."

"To me, also," replied Gabrielle. "Make one move to help her, and I shall destroy this cliff. The three of us will perish." She turned to me and spat out, "I told you there were *two* reasons for my hatred of you. You forgot to ask about the second one."

Frankly, I didn't *care* about the second reason. Whatev-er it was, it wasn't going to convince me that I deserved to die. But maybe if I could keep Gabrielle talking, I could figure out some way to escape. It always worked in the de-tective books I'd read. . . .

"What's the second reason?" I asked politely. My fingers were starting to cramp.

"The second reason is that this—this *cur,* this vile *cur*—became prince of the Drazylvonian vampires through your interference. What *right* had you, a wretched human child, to meddle with vampire laws? Vincenzio had been thrown out of power! He had no right to return to the throne! I will not accept him as my leader—not ever!"

"You chose not to accept me as your leader only because *I* chose not to accept *you* as my partner," said Vincent calmly.

At that Gabrielle began to scream. And even though her voice was a lot louder, nothing she said made any sense to me. When you're holding on to a cliff, it's hard to understand what the people around you are talking about.

"You are not fit to lead our empire! Nor even your measly little brother! No *true* vampire prince would have abandoned me for this—this wretched human child! What has happened to you, Vincenzio? A vampire of your rank, meddling with a *mortal!*"

"As usual, Gabrielle, you are mistaken in every detail," said Vincent. "I abandoned you for no one. I never loved you."

Gabrielle's eyes bulged sickeningly, and she let out a hiss. But Vincent didn't seem to notice.

"In fact, I came to loathe you the longer I knew you. Five hundred years has only strengthened my hatred for you. It is now as strong as iron itself."

Five hundred years! I drew in my breath. I had known that Vincent was ancient, but the thought of him knowing someone for *five hundred years* was beyond my understanding.

"You lie," spat Gabrielle. "You loved me at first sight, and you never ceased to love me. You fell under my spell immediately, and you fled only because you feared the depths of your passion for me."

I should be taking notes on this conversation, I thought. *I'll never hear anyone talk like this again as long as I live.* It was almost enough to make me forget the cold rain and my throbbing hands and the fact that I was poised several hundred feet above some jagged rocks.

"I wonder which of your qualities repels me the most, Gabrielle," Vincent mused. "Is it, perhaps, your vanity? Only you could dream up such a bizarre story. Truly, there was not a vampire in the empire who did not know that I could not abide you."

But Gabrielle wasn't listening. "I was not going to let you leave me in such a cowardly fashion," she snapped. "I vowed to make you confess this love. And then, when at last I found you in Drazylvonia, it was in the company of—of that *object!*" she gestured down at me.

"The thought that a human child had stolen your heart as well as restoring you to power was of course unbearable to me. I had no choice but to destroy her," she went on. Her voice was chillingly reasonable.

"And the film was your route to her destruction?" Vincent asked. "Why such a complicated plan? Why not simply kill her?"

Now there was a definite smirk on Gabrielle's face. "Oh, that would have been too dull. Instead, I determined to enter her life and then decide the most dramatic way of doing away with her." She shrugged modestly. "So I followed her home, where I learned about this stupid little film."

"It's not stupid," I protested feebly. "My dad is a very good writer!" But naturally Gabrielle wasn't listening.

"It was a simple matter to disguise myself as a mortal and win the leading role. What a perfect coincidence to be in a film about vampires! And how satisfying it was to think that I was actually playing the part of the person I would end up killing!"

"It must have been satisfying," Vincent said dryly. "As well as appealing to your vanity. You have always adored being the center of attention. How did you cope with daylight, by the way?"

"Oh, I used a great deal of sunscreen. And I stayed out of direct sunlight, of course. More importantly, I put on the Drazylvonian amulet before leaving for this country."

She plucked the necklace out from under her shirt and showed its silver charm to Vincent. "Wearing this, I have no trouble with the sun."

"*You* stole the amulet?" I had never heard Vincent sound shocked before. "I knew that it was missing. Such a thing has never happened in the history of Drazylvonia! How did you manage to escape with it?"

Gabrielle smiled modestly. "What can I say? It is my little secret. I am a talented person. But amulet or no amulet, Meg was not as easy to kill as I would have liked. And believe me, Meg"— she looked down at me—"I tried many things."

"L-like what?" I quavered. I could hardly bear the pain in my arms now.

"Let me remember . . . Oh, yes. First of all, I fixed the railing on the widow's walk so you'd fall over and locked the door behind you. You are such a clumsy person—"

"I'm not really clumsy!" I interrupted, my face hot with embarrassment. "It's just because I'm growing fast, my mother says!"

Gabrielle gave a meaningful look at Vincent. "Further proof of your insanity. You are in love with a girl who is still under her mother's control."

"He's *not* in love with me!" I protested. "I'm sure he's not."

Gabrielle made an important gesture, as if she were brushing away a fly. "Now, where was I? Oh, yes. You are so clumsy, Meg, that I knew everyone would think you had simply stumbled to your death in your usual clodlike fashion. Except, of course, that you did not die."

"You made it sound as though it were Kilmer's fault," I recalled.

"Of course I did, fool. Have you heard of a lie? Next came my attempt to drown you. I did my best to create a whirlpool in the ocean. Unfortunately, the waters calmed in time for you to be rescued."

"That was my doing," Vincent put in. "I arrived too late to protect Meg entirely, but at least I could stop what you had started."

Gabrielle shot him a look of hatred. "Then the poison I gave you did not work in time."

"So you poisoned the hot chocolate!" I said. "Brooke thought it was Kilmer."

"No, it was I. I concocted a tablet and simply stirred it into your disgusting chocolate as I brought it to you. I confess I still do not understand why the poison did not work. Ingredients in the United States do not work quite the same way as in Drazylvonia. Your herbs are quite inferior to ours."

"Sorry," I said.

"Do not take that tone with me! You are too *nice* to carry it off." She made the word *nice* sound like *cow manure*.

"Speaking of carrying things off, how did you eat during all this?" I asked. "You're the one who attacked Caryl and Mortimer, right?" (That wasn't hard to figure out.)

"Of course I attacked them," Gabrielle said simply. "I felt that both of them needed to be weakened a bit. They were both so loud and selfcentered. Really, drinking their blood was a kindness to them. It made them less tiresome to be around—at least for a few minutes. They will fully recover—regrettably."

"But what did you do the rest of the time?" I asked. "Who else have you been—uh—weakening?"

"Oh, I find that the blood of Americans is also inferior to that of Drazylvonians. I have my own supply shipped to me from home."

That explained those pink diet shakes.

"But enough of this chatter. At last you are mine, Meg—mine to dispose of. When you are out of the way, Vincenzio and I will finally be together. I will share his power. Together, we will rule the vampires of Drazylvonia. And you, Meg, will vanish from my memory like the insignificant dust you are."

She smiled at Vincent—a wild-eyed, feverish smile. "Surely *now* I have brought you back to your senses, Vincenzio?"

My fingers were starting to ache unbearably. I knew I couldn't hold on much longer. But I strained with everything I had to hear Vincent's answer.

His voice was polite, almost regretful. "It is you who are out of your senses, Gabrielle," he said. "I have no romantic interest in Meg."

I told you so, I thought.

Gabrielle laughed delightedly. "So you *do* love me at last! I knew you—"

"Even less am I interested in you," Vincent interrupted. "Hear this, Gabrielle, and believe it. This mortal child—once my sworn enemy—is worth a thousand of you."

Gabrielle's mouth opened wide with surprise and rage, but Vincent went on.

"If I were forced to choose between you—one of my own kind—and Meg," he said, "I would choose her without question. Not that I *plan* to choose her," he added hastily. "It is out of the question. She is immature, and—"

"Hey!" I objected.

"Excuse me, Meg. But I *am* several hundred years older than you," Vincent said, then turned back to Gabrielle. "She is not one of us. But she is braver and more intelligent than you by far."

Now, at last, I knew what Vincent thought of me. And I was glad to know—don't get me wrong. But it was definitely time for me to get off that cliff.

"Vincent," I said faintly, "I could really use some help here. My fingers are just about broken off."

Maybe I shouldn't have drawn attention to myself.

A scream of fury tore out of Gabrielle's throat. It was a sound so dreadful that the memory of it still wakes me up at night now.

She hurled herself down on her hands and knees and lunged over the cliff's edge.

"I *will* kill you, Meg," she said through clenched teeth. "I will tear you to pieces. Then I will throw you piece by piece into the sea."

"No, thank you," I managed to gasp. But she had already grabbed my wrists. And with an insane strength that far surpassed mine, she began to swing me back and forth in the air.

Vincent hurled himself at her, but Gabrielle leaped out of his way. Meanwhile, she was swinging me faster and faster. I knew what she was going to do. She was going to get me going fast enough that I would clear the net when I fell the second time.

The second time there would be no escape. All I could hope to do was to take Gabrielle with me.

With my own last bit of strength I grabbed her wrists so that our arms were locked together. Gabrielle screamed again as she overbalanced. And when I fell, she fell, too.

We bounced into the net—but only for one heart-stopping moment. Then, still clinging together, we flipped over the edge and fell toward the rocks below.

This is it, Gabrielle, I thought. *At least you'll get what you—*

"Meg!" Vincent thundered, hurling himself off the cliff.

Before I had time to wonder how he was doing it, he'd caught me in his arms and was swooping up toward the cliff with me.

Far below us, Gabrielle—now just a vanishing speck of black—howled out, "*I knew it was true!*"

Chapter Twelve

When Vincent got me to the top of the cliff, he set me down rather abruptly.

"You are heavy, Meg," he said, panting.

"Oh, I am not," I scoffed. "I—*Gabrielle!*"

I rushed to the edge of the cliff. Then I froze, my eyes shut tight. Could I really bear to see Gabrielle's mangled form lying on the rocks below?

Well, yes. I could. Steeling myself, I forced my gaze down over the cliff's edge. Vincent was already doing the same thing.

It was almost dark now. The cold gray sea crashed and boomed on the cold gray rocks far below us. One stubborn seagull was struggling to fly straight into the wind, and not having much luck. But there was no sign at all of Gabrielle, living or dead.

"Where is she?" I whispered.

"There is no way to tell," Vincent answered.

"Maybe a wave carried her body away," I suggested hopefully.

"Or maybe she did not hit the rocks at all. She could have turned into a bat and flown off."

"Oh, no," I said, distressed. "She *can't* still be alive. She—" Then I suddenly remembered something.

"Vincent! *You* didn't turn into a bat when you rescued me. It's just as well, I guess, since a bat couldn't have carried me—even though I'm not heavy at all, no matter what you say. But I didn't know you could fly when you're in your, uh, regular form."

"Nor did I," Vincent answered in a rather strained voice.

For a minute I didn't know what to think. "You mean you just jumped down after me?"

Was it possible that Vincent was blushing? *Could* a vampire blush? "Meg, I am not exactly sure what happened. I acted more impetuously than usual. All I know is that suddenly I found myself in the air. Perhaps my cape caught an updraft and returned us here. Perhaps I have more powers than I was aware of, at least when I . . . when I am deeply concerned about something."

Now I was sure he was blushing. But I didn't say anything about it. I didn't want to flutter my eyelashes and say, "You mean, you were concerned about . . . me?" I'm not really the eyelashfluttering type. Also, I wasn't sure I wanted to know *anything* about a vampire blushing. I mean, exactly whose blood does a vampire blush *with!*

The conversation might have gotten even more interesting, except that Vincent suddenly smacked his forehead.

"Gribev!" he groaned. "I forgot that I must pick him up from day care. I was on the way to get him when I sensed that you were in danger. Now his teacher will be wondering what has happened to me. Can I offer you a ride home, Meg?" he added politely.

"That would be very kind, Vincent," I answered with equal politeness. "Because I don't really feel like calling Gabrielle's car service."

Vincent's rental car was black, of course, with a plush gray interior. "It reminds me of a coffin," he explained when he got inside. "Except that few coffins have car seats."

Rain was swirling down the windshield as we drove along, and the countryside looked empty. We didn't talk much, but it was so cozy in the car that I was sorry when we got into town and found Gribev's day-care center.

He was delighted to see us, though. "Vin-vin! Vin-vin!" he squealed when we walked through the front door of the center. He raced to a row of cubbyholes and pulled something out of one. "Look! A puppet!" Proudly he waved a blobshaped piece of black construction paper with Popsicle sticks glued all over it.

"Very nice, Gribev," Vincent said approvingly. "But you have not said hello to Meg. Would you do so, please?"

Gribev ducked his head and smiled shyly up at me. "H'lo, Meg," he said. "Remember when I was a bat, and you fed me milk with sugar in it?"

I smiled back. "I sure do."

"Gribev has *such* an imagination," the teacher said fondly. "He's always talking about being a baby bat back in the old country. Kids! Where do they get these ideas?"

Vincent gave her a strange smile. "Where, indeed?"

"I have to get my things," Gribev said importantly. He marched back to his cubbyhole and pulled out a black raincoat, a pair of black boots, and a stack of artwork.

"We worked on a lot of projects today," said his teacher. "I'm not sure they're all dry yet."

"Splendid," said Vincent vaguely. He winced as Gribev dropped the sticky stack of papers into his hands, but all he said was, "Such wonderful work, Gribev. I cannot wait to inspect it all."

"But how will I *pack* it all?" Vincent asked in dismay when we were back in the car. "It will glue my suitcase closed!"

"Pack?" I said. "You mean you have to leave?"

"I am sorry, but yes." Vincent kept his eyes on the road. "Now that your troubles with Gabrielle are over, I must return to Drazylvonia and resume my normal duties."

"But why? Why can't you just visit for a while? Gribev's happy in day care, and it would be . . . I don't know . . . nice to have you around. We could go to a movie or something." I hardly knew what I was saying. "For once we could just hang around instead of trying to kill each other."

"That would be nice, as you say. But I am a vampire, Meg." Vincent darted a glance at me. "I am not good at hanging around. Except in bat form, of course."

"Not funny," I said in a muffled voice.

He sighed. "No, it was not funny. I wish I could stay. I wish we could become real friends. But it would not be safe for either of us."

Suddenly he veered off the road and pulled the car up onto the shoulder. He turned and looked straight into my eyes. "I can promise you this, however. If ever you need help, I will always be there."

I bit my lip. For some reason I almost felt like crying. "Well, okay. And if ever *you* need help— I will always be here. I don't mean I'll help you with vampire stuff," I corrected myself hastily. "But if you have to go to a conference and you need a sitter for Gribev—for things like that, you can count on me. If I have time off from school, or whatever."

"Thank you, Meg." Vincent cleared his throat. "I will not forget you."

"You'd better not," I said.

I bet you're wondering what happened to the movie?

Everyone involved with the movie certainly wondered what had happened to its star when she didn't turn up for work the next morning. Caryl immediately suggested that Kilmer start the whole film over again, using Caryl as the lead this time around. "I'm very young-looking," she said earnestly. "With the right lighting, I know I could pull it off. You wouldn't have to worry about replacing my part, either. I see Meg as a brave orphan, struggling to face this dreadful danger all by herself. Don't you think that would work a lot better?"

Kilmer didn't. Instead, she called the police, who started a missing-person search. As far as I know, they haven't closed the case yet. But I'm pretty sure they'll never solve it.

I think Mortimer was delighted to have Gabrielle gone. He made a lot of cracks about how unprofessional she was. But even Mortimer shut up when he realized that Gabrielle wasn't going to come back.

And how did Kilmer finally manage to finish *My Babysitter Is a Vampire!*

Well, you may remember my saying that Brooke and Gabrielle looked so much alike that they could have been twins. I was the one who suggested that Kilmer try letting Brooke substitute for Gabrielle in the scenes that still hadn't been filmed. So they fixed Brooke up with a wig and gave her a screen test. To everyone's surprise (especially Mortimer's), she did a great job.

It was a lot of fun watching Kilmer film the rest of the movie. I never did get to be an extra in the beach scene (Kilmer ended up cutting that scene anyway), but I did get to be one in the scene where "Meg" goes to a dance. I'm the one in the lower right-hand corner, dancing with that cute blond guy.

My father got another great screenwriting job right after *My Babysitter Is a Vampire* was finished. This time I told him he was writing it on his own.

My mother and brother had a great vacation.

And I—well, I could finally stop feeling afraid of Vincent. But I couldn't help wondering when— or if—I'd ever see him again. I wondered, too, what had become of Gabrielle. Was she really out of the way for good? Vampires have a way of turning up more than once. . . .

Oh, well. No use thinking about that now.

My Babysitter Is a Vampire.

Coming to television next month. Check your local listings.

Don't miss it!

ANN HODGMAN is a former children's book editor and the author of over forty children's books, including the popular *My Babysitter Is a Vampire* series and the *Stinky Stanley* series. In addition to humorous fiction for children, she has written teen mysteries and nonfiction for reluctant readers. She lives with her husband, two children, and seventeen pets in Washington, Connecticut.

JOHN PIERARD has illustrated the bestselling *My Teacher Is an Alien* series and the *My Babysitter Is a Vampire* series. His pictures can also be found in several books in the *Time Machine* series and in *Isaac Asimov's Science Fiction Magazine*. He lives in Manhattan.